≠
M453p

A PLACE
OF SILVER
SILENCE

ARDATH MAYHAR

ILLUSTRATED BY

PAT ORTEGA

MILLENNIUM

A BYRON PREISS BOOK

WALKER AND COMPANY

NEW YORK

A PLACE
OF SILVER
SILENCE

Dedicated to Ray Peuchner

Cover painting by Pat Ortega
Book design by Alex Jay/Studio J
Book edited by David M. Harris
Special thanks to Barbara Peuchner, Amy Shields, Gwen Smith,
and Mary Higgins
This book may not be reproduced in whole or in part,
by mimeograph or any other means, without permission.
For information address: Walker and Company,
720 Fifth Avenue, New York, NY 10019.

Millennium Books and the Millennium symbol
are trademarks of Byron Priess Visual Publications, Inc.

Library of Congress Cataloging-in-Publication Data

Mayhar, Ardath.
   A place of silver silencc / by Ardath Mayhar; illustrated by
Pat Ortega.
      p.   cm.—(Millennium)
   Summary: Young Andraia fights with the government not to
destroy the planet where she is working alone, because of an
intelligent life form she has discovered there.
   "A Bryon Preiss book."
   ISBN 0-8027-6825-3
   [1. Science fiction.]   I. Ortega, Pat, ill.   II. Title.
III. Series.
PZ7.M468Pl 1988   88-10645
[Fic]—dc19   CIP
                                             AC
Printed in the United States of America

10 9 8 7 6 5 4 3 2 1

Books in the Millennium™ Series

THE LEGACY OF LEHR
by Katherine Kurtz

A DARK TRAVELING
by Roger Zelazny

CHESS WITH A DRAGON
by David Gerrold

PROJECT PENDULUM
by Robert Silverberg

THE FOREVER CITY
by Richard A. Lupoff

THE YEAR OF THE RANSOM
by Poul Anderson

JOE GOSH
by Tom de Haven

A PLACE OF SILVER SILENCE
by Ardath Mayhar

A PLACE
OF SILVER
SILENCE

Link

The theme from Orbeck's *Seven Suns Rising*
sang through the crèche. The bustle of the Nans as
they moved into the dormitories joined the rustle of
movements made by the fourteen children who had
waked to the signal.

Andraia felt her heart thumping hard, almost
making her feel sick, as she swung her feet over the
edge of her sleep-pack and stood beside it, allowing
the facility to roll itself into a neat bundle and flick
back into its niche in the wall at its head. Beyond
Lissia and Fedra, her companions on the segment of
the dormitory enclosed by tapecase walls, she could
hear Josip and Frell and Jorg repeating her motions.

It seemed a perfectly normal day, but it was not.
Besides being her tenth birthday (along with the
birthday of every other of the fourteen in this dorm),
it was also Link-Day. The promised treats, antici-
pated for two years as the Nans prepared their
charges for this all-important day, were forgotten in
the surge of dread. Today she would be Linked to
Josip. Would it be painful?

The Nans said it would not, but they also told
her that the protein gruel was delicious, and her own
tastebuds told her that was very far from being the
truth. How could they know? Kind as they were,
devoted to their charges as they might seem, they

were, after all, artificial beings, incapable of real feeling or the unique sensory perceptions of which human beings were capable.

Anything implanted inside her skull had to hurt. It was only reasonable to believe so, and if nothing else she and her peers had been taught rational assessment of circumstances. So Andraia was filled with well-controlled fear as she donned her coverall (pink for this special occasion) and followed her roommates into the narrow corridor that joined all the segments of the dormitory.

Josip was ahead of her. Though his back was straight, his hair tidy, his demeanor just what the Nans best liked to see, she noted that he was engaged in tying a knot in the back of Jorg's belt, which the boy had not yet buckled. She almost grinned.

Breakfast was a matter of long lines, subdued babble, and pink-iced cakes in honor of the Link-Day of fourteen of the crèche's complement. The younger children regarded these fortunate ones with awe. Those a year or so older smiled reminiscently and said nothing. Andraia envied them. They were already done with this frightening time of their lives. Secure in their life-long linkages, they had no more reason for fear, she was certain.

After breakfast, the children were shepherded off to their daily occupations. Only the fourteen birthday children were kept in the main assembly room, seated in pairs about the round table at its center. The Director himself entered the room as the opening theme from Strauss's *Also Sprach Zarathustra* announced the beginning of the crèche's workday.

Those around the table were silent. Andraia

wondered if anyone else was as tense as she found herself to be. She reached blindly and caught Josip's hand, and his warm fingers closed about hers. She was grateful that they had always been friends, as far back as they could recall. Some of the others to be Linked had not been. That must be even more disturbing at this crucial time.

"Today is a most wonderful day," the Director began. "After today, not one of you will ever be lonely again."

It was the thing the Nans kept saying, over and over, to their young charges. Andraia had never been lonely *before* this. Surrounded by people and Nans as she had been, the thought of loneliness was a bit intriguing. But she turned her thoughts back to the man's speech . . . which sounded as if it had been used many times before.

"From this time forward, your training will change. Your assessments are being run through the computer system now. Your specialties will be assigned in the weeks to come, and your serious training is about to begin. It will be much more interesting when you approach it Linked to someone with the same skills and interests that you have." He paused to look around at the intent faces turned up to him.

"I understand that you are feeling rather shy and afraid, now. It is a natural thing. Faced with the unknown, people always feel so. But I can assure you, nothing will hurt. Nothing will even disturb you. You are about to enter into the most wonderful time of your lives. Believe me. Now go to your Nans. They will take you to the Link-Lab." He stared down at them from his adult height, and Andraia found herself wondering if he had ever been Linked. He looked so sad, for a moment, that it seemed he might have been Linked and lost her.

She rose in unison with the others and followed Nan-one out of the room. It was time!

She went into a washroom with the other six girls. Nan-two was in charge of this group, and she lined them up before the washbasins and clipped the hair away from a spot on each temple as Andraia held herself stiffly to keep from flinching from the scissors. A dab of chilly liquid was pùt on the spots, and she was pushed gently forward. She left the room in a file of pink-clad girls and found herself looking up to see a line of pink-clad boys coming from the other washroom down the hall.

Each had a damp spot on either side of his head. Each looked both stunned and apprehensive. She caught Josip's eye and grimaced. He squinched his mouth in reply.

The speaker above the lab door spoke. Two names. A boy and a girl moved hesitantly together, linked hands, and went through the door, which sighed shut behind them. Andraia drew a long breath. She was trembling. Josip moved to stand beside her. She could feel him trembling, too.

Their turn came too soon. They were the fourth pair to enter the lab. As they found themselves inside, shut away from everyone, they were grasped gently by padded hands and set into chairs that were furry-warm and vibrated soothingly beneath them. They leaned their heads back against the plushy headrests. A voice spoke.

"You are the heirs to a very old, very valuable

ability perfected by the ancestors of those living today. The Link was devised thousands of years ago, using technology that came into being with the prototypes of the computers of today. The chip that will be put into your skulls is akin (though far more sophisticated) to those used in those primitive devices.

"As is the case with so many of the works of men, the chips were first used in warfare. They Linked commanders in the field with their superiors in command posts and the computers, feeding all data directly to them. This allowed an immediate reaction to changing battlefield conditions that had never before been possible. The computers being equal in capacities for reaction and assessment on all sides of any war, the entire matter of warfare became one of stalemate, too expensive to maintain for long periods. This brought about the first lengthy period of absolute peace in the history of humankind."

Andraia had heard much of this before, in history classes. She turned restlessly on the couch, but the voice went on.

"After that use was discarded, the chip was used to Link educators with students, key managerial and technical people in business, those involved in dangerous enterprises with their principals. All of those uses were found to be mutually destructive to their participants, owing to the differences in the adult persons involved. It was found after long study that adults have developed mental barriers, quirks, and habits that make it unfeasible to Link them productively.

"At that point it was decided to make the experiment of Linking human children. The age of ten, being pre-puberty, was chosen as the ideal time for this to be done. The first pairs so Linked were found to attain a ninety-eight percent compatibility with minimal adjustment problems. Growing up together, the Linked pairs formed formidably stable marital units, lacking the distrust and jealousy and sexual dysfunctions suffered by many or most adults forming such a union. Knowing the thoughts of the other, no partner could lack understanding and knowledge.

"You are the lucky recipients of generations of progress in this field. Your lives will be smoother, more useful, and happier than those of anyone denied this wonderful Linkage. It is time, now, for your real lives to begin." The voice died away in a murmur.

Andraia found herself tensing, even amid the comforting ministrations of the couch. Something moved out of a door beside her head. She tried to flinch away, but a ridge she had not known was there baffled the motion.

She felt a light tap on her right temple. At the same moment, something touched her left temple. Neither was painful or even frightening. The couch lifted her to a sitting position again.

"It is done," said the voice, but Andraia was staring at Josip, her mind reeling.

For she saw herself sitting on a couch. She clutched at the plushy upholstery. She was seeing through Josip's eyes!

Josip was looking pale, she saw, when she made her own perceptions return. He was the greenish shade he always turned before throwing up. She jumped down and caught his hand.

"Hurry!" she urged, as they left through the inner door that opened for them, finding themselves in a small washroom with a basin at just the right height for throwing up in. Josip used it to good advantage.

She felt her own stomach heave. She used the adjoining basin.

They left through a door that led into another corridor entirely than the one from which they had entered. A Nan stood there, a smile on her metallic face.

"Come with me," she said. "It takes a bit of time to get used to this new state of things. You need to be quiet together until you learn to control your perceptions. We have a room just for this. Here . . ." She handed each of them a lozenge.

Though neither had any appetite, they took the ruby-colored things politely and popped them into their mouths. The flavor was almost imperceptible, but their rebellious stomachs felt better at once. They followed the Nan into a small cubicle with side-by-side couch-chairs. Those, too, purred comfortingly when they reclined on them.

The door closed behind the Nan. Andraia/Josip closed their eyes. Their minds were a jumble of wonder and remembrance. They lay there for a long while, exchanging thoughts with the timid expectancy of new acquaintances. They found themselves laughing at the same comical recollections.

Andraia let a thought slip into her mind. Josip pounced upon it at once.

"What will they assign us to become?" The question came from both of them simultaneously. "What is it that we can do better than anything else?"

The couches vibrated hypnotically. They relaxed.

10

"I didn't know I was lonely," each said to the other.

They drifted into a dreamlike state, their minds moving into a rhythmic conjunction. When the door opened and Nan-one looked in, they came out of the fog begrudgingly. Never before had either felt so warm, so comfortable, so satisfied.

"It's time for the birthday party," said the Nan. "Time for games and sweets and entertainment. Come, children! Come at once and tidy yourselves."

Now Andraia understood the smiles of those older than she. The offered treats had once seemed too wonderful to think of. Now they paled beside the thing she had found within the pairing of herself and Josip. Other things might come—would come, she knew dimly, with time and maturity.

But for now, to be Linked was a thing so amazing that nothing could be compared. She rose, however, and took Josip's hand. It was warm, and somehow he had managed to get a bit grubby, as usual. That too was a part of the linkage.

She pushed open the door, and the newly made Links went out to begin their life together.

1

Andraia's scream pulled her from the soothing field of the hypnocouch.

"Josip! Oh, no!"

She sat up abruptly, jerking the leads from her nerve endings, her inner vision still seeing that terrible thing that had been done to her Link. Shivering, she huddled her feet beneath her, arms against her chest. Tears trickled slowly down her face as she stared, unseeing, at the steel-gray wall of the Shelter.

Josip! Oh, Josip! she thought.

Behind her eyes, the Thryll were still at work, making an art form of what had been her life's companion. She knew, intellectually, that they had no conception of physical pain. Yet something primitive inside her still wanted to rend and tear those cold aliens as they had rent and torn Josip.

Her teeth were chattering. The couch began to vibrate gently, the velvety texture warming. The quiet, persuasive voice said, "Andraia, we must face your problem squarely. You must let Josip go. There is a life yet to be lived, for you are not yet twenty. Lie down again. Let me help you."

The warmth eased her shaking. Her teeth

stopped their chattering, and her nerves eased. Sighing, Andraia lay back on the hypnocouch.

"I can't let Josip go!" she protested aloud, though she knew the couch was attuned to her thoughts. "He was half of myself for so many years. How can I lose half of me?"

The soft prickles of the leads as they crept again to link with her nerves soothed her a bit. This had become habit, over the past weeks. And there lay before her an entire planetary year in which to regain her ability to function as one of the First Contact teams of the Interstellar Service. An officer who was incapable of meeting alien beings without going into shock was useless to that organization.

"But he *is* gone," said the motherly voice of the couch. "You must accept that. You must accept the thing that was done to him, as well. The Thryll meant no harm. Their own bodies are infinitely adaptable and plastic. They had no conception of the destructibility of the human body. They were shocked and appalled to find that Josip could not reassemble himself, as they can do."

A shuddering sigh came from the girl on the couch. She closed her eyes, feeling the linkages form, stimulating memory centers in her brain. She felt, as well, the terrible emptiness where the implant was . . . the Link that made her one with Josip on their tenth birthday.

The crèche years rolled past rapidly, pausing only when some vital incident had to be replayed in her mind. Seldom was there anything unusual there, under the competent supervision of the Nans and the computers. Only when she and Josip had left that womblike existence for training had things changed for them.

They had been twelve when that happened. Psychoscans had been made of all the children of that age, and they had been assigned to appropriate services. Only Josip and Andraia, of their birth group, were found to be suitable for training as xenologists.

They had gone together into the shuttle that would bear them away to some undreamed-of school, there to be turned into First Contact officers and trained in the skills and disciplines that they would need. Andraia twisted on the couch as the memories unreeled inside her skull. The stress of those intensive years overrode even the tranquilizing effect of the couch.

The leads retracted. "That is enough for today," said the motherly voice. "It is time to go about your duties. Keep your mind focused on your work, Andraia, and on the things I tell you. Only if you let your control slip, returning your memory to that terrible experience, will you begin having the waking dreams again."

Andraia rose from the couch. She shook herself. The overly protective attitude of the couch sometimes irritated her . . . she was quite all right in any normal set of circumstances. Only asleep or faced with an alien intelligence was she devastated by the backwash of the thing that had been done to Josip, and through the Link to her also, by the Thryll.

Here on Argent, she knew that she didn't have

to worry about anything of the sort. The silver-washed world held many sorts of small animals, but no real sapience had been discovered in the intensive sweep the psychsearch machines had given it. She was secure, here, safe from the only thing that terrified her.

2

Outside the Shelter, the land sloped away gently before and rose as gently behind. There seemed to be no rough and tumultuous places or creatures on this quiet world. The vegetation had a silvery sheen, the sky was silvery blue, even the soil was a silver-dun color. Pebbles gleamed like coins underfoot.

A flash of silver-gray fur swooped overhead— one of the flying mammals that served as birds on this reptileless world. The creature uttered no sound as it caught from the ground a scuttering shape and stroked strongly to regain altitude. The captive was silent, as well.

"The quiet will make me well, if nothing else does," said Andraia aloud. The words seemed to boom across the hillside, and she felt somehow embarrassed, as if she had made a social blunder.

Faintly, distantly, she heard a swishing sound. The tideless seas of this moonless planet washed evenly along the shores of the continents, only disturbed by one of the frequent storms. She wondered suddenly if too much peace and quiet might not drive one mad as surely as too much conflict and stress.

She laughed softly. What rubbish!

In her gray jumpsuit, strung around with tools of many strange descriptions, she strode toward the dome that housed the monitors. Into that space, loading into its powerful computer and backup system, went all the data collected by the satellites set into place by the departing shuttle that had brought her here to tend the mechanisms.

In addition, monitoring devices had been set
into the seas, attached to the unobtrusive mountains, placed, in fact, anywhere anything interesting, geologically speaking, might be expected to occur. Some of the native wild animals had also been tagged with sensing collars that put their own information into the growing files.

It was Andraia's duty, among other things, to check the computer, make sure the satellites were functioning properly, count the input monitors to make certain that no element of the planetary survey was missing, and, if that should happen, to go to the location and repair any damage. So far, so quiet had been the tenor of life on Argent there had been no opportunity to do that.

She opened the irising lock that kept out any trace of dust or other contamination. In the far rank of monitors, a light was blinking red. Something was making a high beeping sound . . . it reminded her of the Earthfilm she had seen in the crèche in which a creature called a chick had lost its mother hen.

Feeling a surge of interest at this unexpected problem, she bent over the system. Her diagnostic wand found nothing wrong with the mechanisms. The trouble lay, she was certain, with the device.

She touched a pressure plate, and a map lit on the wall. There. On the shore, some three kilometers from the Shelter.

She had used her flitter once or twice, skimming over the forests, the wide grasslands, and the shallow seas. But she had not walked much in this new place. This was a good opportunity for such an exercise.

She took the weapon, of course. That was standard procedure on any new world, no matter how tame it might seem. But here it was ridiculous. She knew it was ridiculous. Left to her own devices, she would have left the thing in the dome . . . but that was impossible. Along with the Link, she and Josip had found, they had been implanted with a chip that allowed those who taught them to program their minds with the commandments of their profession. One of those was to take a weapon. She sighed and snapped the thing to her tool belt.

The way to the sea lay up that gradual rise of ground. Beyond was a forest that shone in the pale sunlight as if every leaf were lined with silver. She could hear faint motions above her as she walked beneath the trees. Hundreds of species of small animals tenanted Argent. She suspected that thousands more, smaller still, lived in nooks and crannies of this world where predators were unknown.

The forest's floor was clean of undergrowth. These trees must live for uncounted ages, she thought, for she saw no deadfall and no downed timber. Not even the stump of some patriarch of the forest could be seen. All were of similar size and shape. No fire or windstorm had scarred their branches or their boles more than minimally.

In this mild winter season, nuts still littered the ground, each shaped like a silver thimble with tiny indentations rayed along its sides. Among them scurried more small beasts, furred and smooth-skinned and scaled, though she kept reminding herself that no reptilian creatures had been found here.

She strode onward, once she had noted the different species busy among the nuts. The swishing of the sea was growing more distinct, and she wanted to see it on its own level, not from the elevation of the flitter. The one thing on Thryllia that she recalled with pleasure was that world's vast reaches of ocean.

Beyond the forest she found a long level space that was thickly grown with tough grasses. They were of a green so dark that the normal silvery tint was almost lost along the veinings. These grew almost to the water's edge, for there could be no wide tide-washed sands for beaches on such a still world. The solar tides, she had learned, moved the waters too slightly. Only the fierce storms had pounded stone to sand over the aeons to form a neat and narrow hem for the sea.

The waves themselves were tidy and undemonstrative, rippling onto the soil at the shoreline, retreating smoothly to make way for the next. She removed her heavy socks and her boots and tied them onto her belt. Then, barefoot, she splashed along the water's edge toward the silent recording device.

In this mild winter season, nuts still littered the
ground, each shaped like a silver thimble with tiny
indentations rayed along its sides. Among them
scurried more small beasts, furred and smooth-
skinned and scaled.

The breeze was slight. The waves were too polite. She found herself longing, suddenly, for the tumultuous breakers on Thryllia. There had been an excitement about the rushing and pounding of those waters against the granite cliffs she had known there.

She paused, catching at her rib cage. Thryllia . . . the Thryll . . . and Josip, his body opened, not by knives but by three-fingered hands. She still felt in her own body the agony of that ripping.

Andraia bent suddenly and vomited into the curling wavelets. Then, her belly empty, she straightened, wiped her face, and moved away down the waterline toward her goal.

20

3

As she moved southward along the shore, the land grew steeper, until she was walking, at last, beside a considerable cliff. Bedrock had been shifted upward, she thought, by gradual tectonic movements. She could see no sign of dramatically sudden events . . . the layers of soil and rock were even as the leaves of a book.

She noted those layers, as she went, speaking into her pocket link with the computer. From time to time she saw very strange indentations, however, seemingly marked onto the few smooth sandstone faces she found. They formed dots in unusual patterns, which recurred with some regularity. If she had not known better, she would have thought the markings to be some sort of written code or language.

As she rounded a gradual curve of the cliff, she found one immense face, on which had been cut [.:..··], not once but several times. She felt her heart grow chill. That was no random act of wind and weather. Such precise repetitions spoke of minds and hands . . . alien ones. She shivered uncontrollably for a moment. Then she set her teeth and spoke again into the computer.

"There is a set of markings on cliff above, latitude thirty-nine degrees eight feet eleven inches north, longitude one hundred seven degrees three feet nine inches east. Not natural. Though small, they are dug deeply into the sandstone. The weathering at edges suggests some years of aging. I see no chisel marks . . . Some pointed tool—sharp stick or stone, I would say—was used." Her voice had begun to shake, and she snapped off the link and sat on a bit of fallen sandstone.

Aliens . . . were there aliens here too, in this place the Service had chosen as a safe haven for her healing? She clenched her teeth, hugged herself, head down, as she battled for control.

She was alone with the problem; that was the worst thing of all. Not only was she cut off, permanently and without recourse, from Josip, she was also cut off from any other person in her Service, as well. Communications with the nearest Base required thirty-two hours by superlight transmission, which was used only in emergencies. Regular transmissions of data required three years.

Now she was shaking uncontrollably. Her memory fled back to Thryllia, to the initial contact, when the Thryll had seemed so delighted to find another intelligent kind. Josip had been delighted. She had set to work at once, gathering material for their reports. He had gone, as was his habit, to program the Translator and to talk with the Thryll. Their constantly changing bodies had fascinated him, as did the colors that flowed through them and denoted their moods and shades of meaning.

She was busy with the monitors, preparing them for setting about the new world on which the pair of them would work for the next two years. Josip had dimmed his linkage with her, to avoid distraction as he studied the speech patterns presented by the Translator. She usually lost herself in her work, anyway, and so she had been unaware of the situation leading up to the sudden burst of agony that had caught her unawares.

At first, she had thought herself ill with some sudden, alien disease. Her stomach felt as if it were being torn apart, and her ribs felt strained, as if some hand were pulling the bones apart.

She retched as she slid from her chair to curl in fetal position on the floor of the Domicile. She felt blood flowing . . . she managed to look, yet her own flesh was untouched.

Then she knew that it was not her own pain she felt—it was Josip's. She let her senses flow into her Link. If she must suffer, she had to know why and what was happening to him.

She had stared up into the sparkles that were Thryll eyes, set in the constantly remolding putty of their upper portions. Scarlet and golden streaks flowed over and through the metamorphosing bodies that loomed against the brown-green of treetops and the purple of the evening sky. Even as she watched, an extruded pseudopod rose into view, holding a coil of looping gut . . . Josip's entrails . . . which was twined into a rosettelike shape. And then a hand reached her heart—or Josip's, for it made little difference.

There was an unutterable surge of pain. And then there was nothing.

Sitting on the sandstone of this distant world, she felt again the blankness of her awakening from the long unconsciousness that had followed Josip's death. She had thought herself dead too, for a time.

It was dark, of course, and for a long while she could not focus enough to see the tiny twinkles of green and blue that marked the activity lights of the equipment. Her head felt as if some part of it had been forcibly removed . . . there was a hollow space filled with aching loneliness.

There was no more pain, not of the sort that had killed her Link, but her body ached all over as if she had been beaten. It had taken hours for her to make herself move, days to make herself begin to eat, to send the emergency signal that would bring help, and to take up the bare necessities of living again.

She made herself inhale deeply. She stood, still shaking, and stretched her muscles until they would work properly again. She must check the inactive equipment. She must return to the Dome before dark and make her daily report for sublight transmission. She must continue to live, no matter what terror racked her. She had her duties, no matter what personal travail she might have to overcome in order to perform them.

4

The inoperative sensor had been placed in a crevice in the cliff wall, well above the tops of any waves that might be sent lashing against the shore by storm winds. She followed the telltale, which beeped more and more shrilly as she neared the location of the device. She found it at shoulder level, when she stood on an outcrop of harder stone that lay like a shelf at the foot of the sandstone layer.

She took the diagnostic wand from her tool belt and moved it along the length of the stavelike sensor. When she read the result, she did it again, even more carefully. The answer was the same . . . the sensitive button at the end of the thing had been detached.

She stepped back onto the beach. She was shaking again, very quietly, but her mind was clear. Only hands could detach that button . . . it screwed onto the threaded end of the device. She had to see if it had been left with the rest of the piece, down in the cranny. She stepped up, grasped the edges, and pulled herself up the rockface, finding a toehold in a small ledge.

The button winked at her from the V-shaped bottom of the nook. She managed to get her hand into the crack, working her fingers down to grasp the thing between her fore and middle fingers. Once she had replaced it, she climbed back down shakily and stood beside the water, thinking hard.

Was she, even now, being observed by enemy eyes? Would all her emplacements be disabled as this one had been? Was she doomed to move over and over this world, repairing and replacing, at the mercy of whatever alien beings had marked those enigmatic dots into the sandstone wall?

She was shivering again, but now she was in control. The weeks with the hypnocouch had only reinforced her own determination to bring herself back to normal. Josip would not have wanted her to become disabled because of the thing he had suffered, and she refused, on her own account, to let her mental condition disrupt her work.

She set off up the shore again, her bare feet now chilled as they moved. The wind was freshening to seaward, cooling. It was, after all, winter on Argent. She stopped as soon as she cleared the cliffs and moved inland to put on her boots.

As she rose from her crouch, she had a sudden strange sensation . . . something warm pulsated beneath her hand. A tingle of pleasure went through her . . . this was a memory, but one she found hard to trace back to its source. Then she had it.

A group of psychologists had come to the crèche with various tests for the children. With them they had brought the first living animals any of the youngsters had ever seen . . . a tiny goat, a miniature horse, a pig, a dog, and a bored tomcat who had watched the proceedings with jaundiced eyes. He had, however, loved being stroked.

Now Andraia recognized the sensation . . . it was the same she had felt when running her timid hand over the plushy fur of the blue-gray cat. She recalled the vibration of his purr, as well. Was that where they got the idea for the hypnocouch's characteristics?

She thumbed the homing button of her directional device. Might as well cut across country—it was becoming too chilly to walk along the shore any longer. This took her into a different segment of the forest, approaching her Shelter's location from the southwest.

The trees were now dark against a rapidly darkening sky. The silver overcast that had come with sunset was turning plum-colored, and she flicked on her power-beam and moved onward, hoping to reach her goal before it became fully night. Above her, she could hear movement in the treetops. Scritchings as of tiny claws grasping at bark. Sharp intakes of breath, as if some voiceless, arboreal creature were frightened by her presence.

The light seemed to lose itself in the duff of the forest floor, and she was picking her way cautiously along over the uneven terrain when she caught a glitter from the corner of her eye. Ruby-colored, it flashed, blinked out, flashed again.

She paused and shone her beam in that direction. A pair of eyes glowed over a low branch. She could see silvery fur tufted about them and a dim shape mingled with the winter leaves of the limb to which it clung. She moved closer . . . such a small, helpless creature couldn't possibly pose any threat to her.

The branch was just above head height. She looked up, keeping the light angled so as not to blind the animal. Its fur shone silver in the intense beam, and its eyes blinked convulsively, as if it were terrified.

"That's all right, little one," she crooned soothingly. "Are you lost? Are you all right?"

The small creature seemed to lose its grip on the bark. With a shivering of leaves and fur, it fell into her hands. She caught it reflexively, though she knew that touching unfamiliar beasts on alien worlds was a thing frowned upon in all the manuals she'd ever seen. But she couldn't let such an innocuous creature hit the ground.

The fur was warm in her hands. She cuddled the small one to her breast, feeling its heart pound in a strange trip-hammer rhythm. It was frightened. She couldn't leave it in the night-bound forest, whether or not there were supposed to be predators on Argent.

The quivering began to diminish. She felt the pointed chin dig into her collarbone, the tiny hands grasp her jumpsuit's collar. The furred creature climbed onto her shoulder and tucked itself beneath her chin.

She set her power-beam in its holder at her belt, focused on the ground just ahead of her feet. With both hands stroking the plushy fur of her new friend, she moved through the forest, her fears of aliens

Its fur shone silver in the intense beam, and its eyes blinked convulsively, as if it were terrified.

forgotten in delight at finding this animal. She had needed something living with which to share her life. If it would remain with her . . . if it would thrive in her environment . . . then she would have, for the first time in her short life, a real pet all her own.

5

Andraia would have liked to sleep, that night, with the furry beast cuddled against her. She knew, however, how foolhardy that would be; she must know its habits and disposition before risking such closeness. It settled into a pod from which electronic equipment had been removed and curled its tail, which was sinuous with a wispy fluff of fur at the end, over its pointed nose. She stroked it until it relaxed.

She studied the animal closely as it lay there. The eyes, though small, had markings around them that gave the illusion of greater size. There were shadow markings among the whiskers, giving it more expression than was usual with an animal. She remembered the otterlike smoothness of its motions in the trees . . . it was truly unlike any animal she knew, yet it had traits similar to some that she had studied.

The small hands clenched. The eyes closed, and the silvery-furred chest heaved in a sigh. There were three layers of fur—she riffled it as she stroked—the lower ones very pale yet possessing color, ochre and bluish tints, and the topmost a subtle silver.

She turned away, finding that she resented the

time she must spend on the hypnocouch. She wanted to make the acquaintance of her new pet. She knew she must follow the prescribed course of healing, however, and she went off to the tiny chamber where the couch was hooked into the computers for her daily session.

She lay back and felt the leads creeping into her pores, finding nerve endings, tickling her scalp as well. She allowed the pain of the day before to rise to the surface of her consciousness. Never before had she let the couch deal with the direct agony of her loss.

The velvety surface pulsated, reminding her of the rhythmic quivering of the little animal she had found. She relaxed, and the remnant of the Link connected her with the mind of the computer controlling the couch. All her pain and loss ran away along the microscopic pathways leading to the control centers of the hypnocouch. She knew that they would return, but for the moment she felt relief.

The voice spoke softly into her consciousness. "Pain cannot last forever. Loss dims with time. You are young, Andraia. You are strong. You are bright and well-trained. Loose the memories. Forget the wounds you suffered with Josip. Let him go, child; let him go and find peace."

She felt her eyelids grow heavy. The voice smoothed her anxieties, leading her into sleep. Even as she went under, she felt beneath her hand the pulsating of the couch, the plush of its upholstery. Or was it the body of the little animal? But she was adrift on an inner sea and could not say which it might be.

She was rocking gently on an ocean. Josip was beside her, his head turned away as he watched a sea bird fly overhead. She recognized one of the Thryllian gulls, and she wondered what strange illness might have made her dream so terribly of losing him, of losing herself. Then she wondered . . . why was she afloat on the ocean of Thryllia? She and Josip had never ventured onto those stormy waters, separately or together.

The thought almost pulled her from the trance, but the couch murmured soothingly, and she went under again.

Josip's fair head turned toward her. His eyes, gray-green, slightly worried, as always, were regarding her intently. His hand reached toward her, and she took it in chilly fingers. Why did he look so sad?

"This is a fantastic world," she said.

The gull swooped low over them, its black neck stretched long, its scarlet eyes staring as it examined these intruders into its watery realm. It squawked raucously and banked to climb again.

"It was a fantastic world. The people were fantastic people, plasmoid, three-fingered, artistic. I died, Andraia, in the pursuit of their art. Believe this. They honored me past my worth. I knew it, even as I suffered. You would have too, if you had not been struck so suddenly by the pain, without any preparation."

She struggled to rise from the dream, once she recognized it for such, but the couch held her inexorably. "You *are* dead? I didn't dream it? The Thryll did those terrible things to you? Josip!" Her wail was carried away by the rising wind.

His voice was deep, musical as always. "Don't misunderstand, Andraia. I did not die purposely. I had no premonition of danger when I agreed to participate in the Thryll ritual, even though I had seen three of the Thryll themselves rearranged into the patterns they find most beautiful. They had resumed their shapes by degrees, once the ritual moved past them." He sighed.

"I made an unwarranted assumption, and I died for it. I thought they had understood what the Translator had told them about our bodies and our minds, our culture and our technologies. But they had not, for the Thryll have no straightforward narrative techniques. Everything they say is couched in metaphor and hyperbole. Nothing is exactly as it is expressed or as it seems.

"They misinterpreted information that was not subject to interpretation. And when I realized that, it was too late. To resist at that point, to make unseemly outcry, would have been to sacrifice any credibility our kind would ever gain with those people. I died, Andraia. I died. And you were left alone."

"Alone." The word came out as a moan, and the girl struggled from the hypnosis and opened her eyes to the tiny Shelter room.

Something rubbed against her side, climbed up her rib cage to snuggle against her chest. The animal? How had it freed itself from its podlike cage?

She stroked it absently, still seeing Josip against a background of foam-created green-gray waves and sullen sky. But the furry beast did not intend to share her attention with anything. It snuggled beneath her fingers, undulating, vibrating. She remembered the tomcat's lazy purr . . . this was the same effect, although achieved in a different way.

Behind her eyes, Josip turned his face to hers, very near . . . she could almost feel his breath on her cheek.

"Let me go, Andraia! Let me go. Let me go! You will destroy yourself if you cling so tightly to the Link we shared. It is broken. Oh, let me go!"

She sat, tearing the leads from her skin and hair once more. It was the couch. She knew it to be the couch. Yet she felt that Josip had been there, near enough to touch. Near enough to show her the pain in his eyes.

She heaved a shuddering sigh. The animal crept up on her shoulder, holding with its tiny, humanlike hands, and tucked its head beneath her chin.

Strangely comforted, she stroked it again, clearing her mind of the aftermath of the hypnotic session. The pain she had felt for so long was diminished. It definitely was less than it had been. Would she, then, be healed, after all, of the trauma she had carried with her for almost a year?

6

She went about her duties, once the session was sufficiently suppressed to allow that, in an unusually good mood. She attributed that to the fact that her new pet rode on her shoulder as she checked the monitors, did routine maintenance of the mechanisms that provided power for the Shelter and the Dome. She noted a blip up the coast, as she activated the equipment. That might be a problem, or it might be a momentary malfunction. She made a mental note to recheck later.

She found herself talking to the wordless— voiceless?—creature. A name . . . she needed a name for it. That long-ago tomcat had been called Spike, she remembered. But that was no name for such a timid, helpless creature as this. That had been a proper name for a combat-torn veteran of many feline battles and matings. She didn't even know the sex of this beast. Or did its kind have differing sexes?

She persuaded the small creature to curl into her arms. She ran a finger down its soft stomach, parting the fur to show darker layers beneath the silvery outer one. Awkwardly, she peered at the lower part of its anatomy. It was completely smooth. No genitalia appeared to exist . . . at least outwardly.

"What should I call you?" she asked.

It squirmed ecstatically, pressing its furry flesh against her skin. She set it on her shoulder again. The tail curled beneath her chin, the hands grasping her ear for balance.

Andraia smiled. "Love. I shall call you Love."

But she knew that she could not keep the wild creature for long. It should be in its forest. She had no idea what it might eat, and she didn't dare offer it human food. The metabolisms had to be wildly different. No, she must return it to the forest.

Once the work about the Dome was done, she set out on foot for the southwest. When she was over the long ridge of hills that separated the small valley in which her quarters had been placed from the grasslands beside the ocean, she could see the wood ahead. Dark masses of winter leaves shadowed it, though the pale sun shone fitfully between showers of misting rain.

She reached it more quickly than she expected . . . the darkness had slowed her, the night before. When she was beneath one of the trees, she found a low-hanging branch and set the animal atop a fork. It looked surprised and dropped into her hands again. Its small mouth opened as if in protest, but no sound came out beyond a faint gasping noise. She recognized the sound she had heard in the darkness. The trees must swarm with its fellows, and all had been frightened by her passing.

She held the small one in careful hands. "Look, you need to go back up there. I don't know what you eat. I can't take care of you properly. Won't you run back into the tree and find your family?"

Love clambered up the branch a short distance. He pulled loose a patch of fungus and stuffed it into his mouth until the furry cheeks were distended. Then he descended again into her hands, a satisfied expression on the pointed face.

"That's what you eat?" she asked. "Thank you."

She pulled a handful of the stuff, stripping it down the switch from which he had taken his snack. It came easily and was crisp and faintly yeast-scented when she held it to her nose. She filled a pocket of her jumpsuit with it, while Love watched interestedly.

When she was done, the creature gave a sniff and tucked himself under her chin again. "You certainly seem to be a bright little fellow," Andraia said. "Extremely bright for someone who never saw people before."

She made her way back to the Dome and the flitter. The animal made no protest when she climbed into the cockpit and closed the hatch above them. Even when the solar engines began their faint humming, Love didn't show any sign of apprehension.

The machine rose lightly from its grassy pad and skimmed over the forest from which they had just come. Andraia could see the ocean, now, heaving in silver billows as far as her gaze could reach. It melded with the sky at the horizon, and no sea bird flew here. There was no hint of Josip in the cool winter air.

She went higher, banking to skim the shoreline and heading north along the coast. Her telltales indicated the markers as she flew over them. Each seemed intact and active until she came to the one that had alerted her to trouble, when she checked the Dome. That was some fifty kilometers from her base, and behind the coastal plain was a firm area of grass that would provide good landing and takeoff for the flitter.

Between the plain and the grass was a small wood consisting of miniature trees that were bare of the winter leaves most other trees on Argent possessed. When she walked into this wood, carrying Love on her shoulder, Andraia was startled to see every branch occupied by one of her companion's kind.

They made, of course, no sound. But their small hands were busy . . . their motions were graceful, intricate, and indubitably meaningful. Love leaped from her shoulder to climb into a treeful of his fellows. At once he sat upright and began making the hand motions, obviously in reply to those directed at him.

She watched, stunned, as a long "conversation" took place in the tree. The others, sitting in their own trees, watched, too. From time to time one would make a motion to his own group, as if commenting on the hand-talk between Love and the others.

Andraia felt a twinge of uneasiness. If these were intelligent, then they were, by definition, aliens. Sapient aliens. The old terror rose in her, choking her, making her heart thud heavily. Aliens . . . Josip!

As if he felt her physical reaction, Love leaped back onto her shoulder. He curled beneath her chin, and she could not find it in her to be afraid of such a gentle creature. She looked up to find all the others of this strange sort of alien staring down at her with remote expressions, as if they were assessing her and making some sort of judgment.

She controlled herself. Love's vibrations helped in that, as did his warm body pressed firmly against her.

"I am a friend," she said. She doubted that they heard . . . why should they hear if they could not speak?

7

It took several hours to walk to the coast and 4 3 find the inactive sensor. Again, the button had been removed and laid near the device. This time it was very difficult to reach, even with the magnet-tipped tool provided for fishing metal parts from deep places.

Andraia was frustrated and sweaty by the time she had fished and dropped and fished and dropped the button a dozen times. Love, strangely, had not interfered, though he was obviously curious about her actions. He cocked his small head, watching intently, but he never intruded himself between her and her work. And when the button finally came into her hand, he rubbed his head gently against her knee as if in congratulation.

As she flew back to base, Andraia found herself wondering why this small being had come to her. The more she thought, the more she realized that her encounter in the forest had been no accident. Love, she now began to think, had felt her approach in some esoteric way and had put himself into her path. He had literally fallen into her hands, and he had shown no sign of wanting to leave her to return to his own kind.

Motivation . . . she had to find the motivation. There were many ways in which alien beings could prey upon mankind, and some were very subtle, indeed. Some, of course, resulted in a sort of symbiosis, beneficial to both species. But those were rare.

Many more found subtle ways to siphon energy or material things or even technological designs and concepts from the restless human beings with whom they came into contact. She recalled the Shreft, who had pirated ideas directly from the minds of those engaged in trade with those golden-scaled beings. The Shreft had seen possibilities that even the thinkers had not yet considered and had gone into competition that had put the company involved into precarious financial condition for years.

And that had been a non-technological race that had only intelligence and ingenuity and limitless energy as its capital.

Love vibrated gently against her shoulder, as if sensing her disquiet. What injury could this little creature do to her, even if it desired to? That was the question that kept her thinking furiously all the way back.

She retired early and went to the hypnocouch with her problem. Sometimes the therapy cleared her thinking and brought into focus ideas that had been dormant or hidden from her conscious mind.

The couch, responding to the shift in her emotional orientation, did nothing to recall her lost Link to her mind. Instead, it soothed her into total relaxation. Then the computer began taking the facts her mind presented to it and making comparative analyses.

"Pain. That is the common element," said the motherly voice, at last. "You were in pain when you came through the forest, still feeling that traumatic loss you had relived on the beach. Here, when you relived it still again, the creature contrived to escape its cage and come to you. It is not certain, as yet, for there is not enough information on a long-term basis, but it is possible that psychic or physical pain in some manner attracts these beings."

Andraia lay on the pulsating velvet, allowing her mind to absorb the concept. Did Love and his kind find some sort of satisfaction in her pain? Or did they find it so painful to themselves that they had to try to assuage it?

She knew that she had to find the truth, for this discovery must be reported, as did everything else discovered here. However, she did not intend to send incomplete and possibly inaccurate data through the sublight transmissions. She needed empirical tests that proved, one way or the other, what the link might be between herself and this insignificant bundle of fur.

What test might she try, to ascertain some part of it?

She shivered. Pain was, of course, the principal linkage, so far. She understood, then, what she must do.

She put into the pod enough of the fungus to sustain Love for a long while. She had cupped water from a spring in the wood, and she put a container inside, as well. Then she sealed the little being into the pod as securely as was possible, considering that she had to keep open the grid of metal that allowed technicians to check the equipment that was usually kept inside.

Love must, after all, have air to breathe. She had felt the heaving of his small lungs as she held him. She looked down into his triangular face before shutting off the lights in the lab portion of the Shelter. He seemed comfortable. Even as she watched, he curled about and covered his nose with his tail fur.

She went into her own sleeping quarters and closed the door, though she did not latch it inside. She always read for a time before sleeping, so she picked up a book, after she came from the cleansing booth. The *Manual for Xenological Study* did not hold her attention tonight, but she plowed through the lines, even though her mind was anyplace except inside the case histories presented in that useful volume.

When the chronometer read 0200 hours, she rose and went to her storage cabinet. Inside was an assortment of tools she often needed while working about the Shelter. There she kept, also, the only thing she still possessed that had belonged to Josip.

She took from the top drawer of the cabinet a medallion of dull golden metal. In its center was a tiny chip of shining stuff. This had been the amplifier that made the Links work over long distances

. . . her own lay beneath it, but she didn't lift that one from the drawer.

Clasping the thing in her hand, she returned to her couch and lay down. The metal warmed in her hands, as she lay with it clasped over her heart.

Josip! Josip!

For the first time, she deliberately summoned the agony of those last moments of his life. She returned to her station, felt the sudden pain . . . she went back into that world of the Thryll and that death that had been as vivid as her own real death could ever be.

8

Andraia gasped, curled again into that fetal ball.
She saw those color-shot faces changing above her
once more. She was a lump of anguish and loss as
the hands moved in her body, toward her heart.

There came a sound at the door, but she was
too lost in her pain to realize it for a moment. A
thudding, soft and determined, turned into motion
as the door opened and a silver-furred body shot
through to land against her shoulder.

Then Love was burrowing under her hands,
against her breast, his body throbbing with intensity. He lay, at last, clasped to her, his warmth, his
vibrations soothing her, removing the sharp edge of
that terrible ordeal. Nothing touched her mind—she
was alert to that, and years of being Linked made
her sensitive to such mental intrusion. But he knew
the pain—that reached out to touch the little creature in a compelling way.

Andraia felt the easing all through herself. Even
in her mind, where that broken Link seemed to be a
well of emptiness, she felt a lessening of the grief.
No thought was there . . . just a simple physical
touch that seemed to draw out the pain as a poultice
draws the poison from an infection.

She hugged Love to her gently. Although she had no proof, as yet, that would satisfy the rigid requirements of her superiors, she knew it was her pain that had drawn the animal to her. It could not bear such sensations . . . was that a trait carried to the other life-forms on Argent? Or was there something peculiarly compelling about human pain that touched a sensitive wavelength in the furry tree dwellers?

As the terrible sensations receded, her mind cleared even more. This was proof, she knew, though not enough. Now she must find if these creatures truly communicated, and that was going to be a task worthy of even the most experienced officer among her teachers.

Argent was slated to become a testing site for especially dangerous weapons. If Love's kind proved to be intelligent, the law would forbid such uses . . . or any uses at all . . . of this world. Even colonization would be forbidden. There were too many earthlike worlds circling the uncountable stars to allow stealing one from its rightful tenants.

Something hot and bright kindled inside her. She had been trained for this very work. The Thryll had frightened her almost to the edge of her ability to recover. Love seemed to be healing that wound, reestablishing her ability as a xenologist.

If her pain could command her cure, what would be the result of bringing other troubled people here? Could all the furred ones learn to interact with people in pain? And could—or would—they try to heal?

50

She sighed and rose from the couch, holding Love carcfully. He was almost asleep, now that she had eased. His filamentlike whiskers quivered with his breath, and his eyes were half closed.

She took him back and laid him in his pod, where he curled into a deep sleep at once. She stood staring down at the being who seemed so much like an animal but might be so much more. She bent closer, looking intently at a pattern of clawmarks in the paint of the pod's interior.

Love must have waked, bored, before being summoned by her anguish. Tiny scratches repeated that enigmatic symbol she had found on the sandstone cliff face: [.:..··] was unmistakably imprinted in the steel-gray enamel.

She recalled something of the ancient code that had been included in her training. It wasn't precisely the same, but it was the nearest thing she could find to making sound of the markings.

"Di-dah-di-di-deet-deet," she said aloud. "The Deet? It will make it easier to refer to them, when I make my reports. And my reports are going to make some kind of history, I suspect, when I finally decide the data may be sufficient."

She turned again to her bed, but she lay awake for a long while, feeling about inside herself where the festering sore that had been Josip's loss was beginning to heal. It was tender, still, that was true. Yet the unbearable edge was no longer there. The void in her mind was being filled, not with thought or another's perceptions, but with something.

She closed her eyes. The muted clicks and

whirs of the mechanisms that made the Shelter function were hardly discernible in the silence. Nothing on Argent cried or howled or chirped or croaked. It was a place of silence . . . silver silence. A place for rest and healing.

9

Andraia found time, between her rounds of duty, to look into the tapes dealing with communication with alien intelligences. That proved to be less than useful . . . they all assumed that verbal communication would be possible and the Translator could be used. Or they assumed that those aliens were of somewhat similar physical types, having remotely similar needs and wants.

There was nothing that she could find to help in communicating directly with a small furry creature, sexless as far as she could see, though she thought of Love as *he* simply from habit, that lived in trees and had no voice and no ears.

She recalled reading, back in training, a treatise on ancient Earth, where DNA alteration and micro-surgical techniques had not yet reached the level for correcting every human ill. There had been deaf people there. Blind ones, too. Specific techniques had been devised for helping them to function. If she could only find something in the computer system dealing with such obsolete concepts . . . but of course she didn't. What need had a xenologist for such matters?

With Love riding on her shoulder, she went to

the Dome to make her evening check. A light was blinking . . . across the western ocean, on the small landmass in the southern quadrant of that body. Tomorrow would require a demanding journey.

Tonight, however, she had an overriding purpose. It was time for the sublight transmission to go out. She intended to request a relay in micro of a manual of sign language and send it in an ftl burst. It was unorthodox, that was true, and perhaps would bring a reprimand, but she felt a compulsion to do it. Even as she coded the request, she realized that the system of symbolism she had seen had a lot in common with the ancient system called braille. While Love wasn't blind, such a code might be a handy one to possess.

She knew that Fender, at the other end of the long com-link, was going to be shocked. He was a by-the-book officer, always correct, always resistant to unusual situations and circumstances. He was going to kick about this. She added to the coded message: MOST URGENT. NEED SOONEST. MOST URGENT.

The repetition was never used unless the request was of vital importance. He'd kick—but he'd find, somehow, the material she needed, and he would send it at last over the superlight system reserved for urgent messages. He'd grumble. He'd turn it in to his superiors with a recommendation for investigation, but he'd send what she needed.

She laughed softly, seeing in her mind the ginger freckles, the sandy hair in its usual untidy tuft, the severe gray eyes that disapproved of anything he couldn't find in the basic manual. Alex Fender just might find himself *in* his precious book, if this worked out as she suspected it might.

Love was sitting on the back of her neck, his fringed tail curving beneath her chin. He watched what she did as she activated the sublight transmitter, fed in the codes and the tapes automatically produced by the various sensors and the computer. She had the feeling, so tense was his small body as he stared at her hands and the flickering lights of the mechanism she used, that he was memorizing every move she made.

The transmitter began its chirping signal, and Love jumped slightly. Did that mean he could hear? Then she saw that the patterns of lights had also changed drastically, something she had known but never consciously noticed. Which had startled him?

She sighed. It wasn't going to be easy to learn exactly what his reactions reflected. What his capabilities were. What possible common ground she would be able to find that would give them some basis for understanding.

The transmission on its way, she turned to ascertain the exact position of the inactive sensor. She marked her portable computer-connected map with a light pen and went out to install it in the flitter. That would take her directly to the seat of the problem, as soon as she completed the morning duties.

It was dark, of course, and moonless, but the stars were brilliant in the velvety sky. Strange constellations that she was mapping in her spare time

55

were sprinkled across the heavens in intricate patterns.

Across the north, just above the treetops, one of those patterns leaped to her attention. Out of alignment, true, but still recognizable was a parade of stars: [.:...]

She touched Love, took him into her arms. Stretching her arm, she pointed toward the constellation, turning his pointed chin up with a finger so that his eyes would follow her gesture. He went very still.

Then his small hand came up to echo her gesture. Pointing with one hand toward the stars, the furry creature tapped her cheek with the other. It was an approving gesture . . . it reminded Andraia of the way the Nans would sometimes pat a cheek of a child who had done something very intelligent and praiseworthy.

If she understood correctly, Love was congratulating her for being smarter than he thought she was.

Chuckling, she made her way through the star-sprinkled darkness to the Shelter. She had never had a pet. She had never needed such companionship. Since the age of ten she had had Josip, sharing her thoughts, her life, and, once they were matured enough, her body. Such linkage filled every need. Now she realized that Love was filling one small corner of the terrible gap left in her life by the loss of her Link.

She smoothed his fur as she walked. Her feet had learned every unevenness in the grassy space

She touched Love, took him into her arms. Stretching her arm, she pointed toward the constellation, turning his pointed chin up with a finger so that his eyes would follow her gesture. He went very still.

between the Shelter and the Dome. She looked up at the stars, feeling a unity with the small being that she had not known before. He too looked at the stars and thought about them and repeated the pattern of that splendid grouping.

Could his kind have given themselves a sort of coded name, using that design? So the Deet would be, if she had interpreted it correctly, the People of the Stars.

She had the sudden conviction that she was right. These were a new intelligent people. If she could prove it, she was going to confound the Society of Xenologists, the Service, and perhaps infuriate the Powers That Be who intended devastating things for the world they called Argent.

10

Love refused to stay in a tree hung with his favorite fungus food. He refused to remain in his pod. He could, of course, make no outcry, but his little face seemed frantic when she tried to leave him behind.

It was totally against regulations. Alex Fender would have gone into shock at the notion. But Andraia found herself in the flitter with Love tucked into a cranny she padded with an old tunic. He showed no fear as they moved silently over the neat waves, heading toward the waver of silver-sea-on-silver-sky that marked the horizon.

The satellite readout showed a weather cell moving down from the northwest at a rather slow rate. She tuned the audio warning to the signal, so that even if she became engrossed in something else a change in the position of the storm relative to her own would be announced to her at once. The sky was its usual silvery blue. Strands of cobwebby cloud streaked across the northern half, and the sea below held unusual greenish tints.

"We're going to have a storm," she said to Love. By no flicker of change did he indicate that he had heard her voice, but he reached a small hand across from his niche to touch her lips.

They moved over the water at deceptive speed, there being nothing to serve as a measure of their motion. Andraia touched the plate that activated the scanner beneath the flitter. To do an in-depth recording of the ocean floor from such a low altitude would tell geographers and geologists much more than would the satellite version. The screen on her monitor reflected those findings at a touch of her fingers, and she found herself looking down at a broad plain, studded from time to time with what were probably fangs of rock.

Love cocked his head and stared intently. From time to time he twitched his filamentlike whiskers, and his attention didn't waver until she flicked off the monitor. Then he curled down into her old tunic and fell asleep, while she checked data from all the sensors the flitter possessed, sending bursts of transmission back to the computer in the distant Dome.

She was headed southwestward, and the hours moved as slowly as the featureless ocean below her seemed to do. She was pacing the sun, adding hours to her day, and she grew weary at last. When the sun set, the flitter would proceed on stored power until sunrise again. The tremendously powerful and extremely compact batteries used in the machines could power them for days, when fully charged as hers had been by the weeks of sun.

She slept and woke, checked data, transmitted bursts to the Dome, played with Love, and sometimes plugged in the leads that activated the part of her brain that had her favorite music stored in it. Though it was nonselective, she could always enjoy the minutely recalled harmonies of Martian wind music or Mozart concerti or Sylestrian serenades.

So the time passed, and on the fourth day she thought she saw a darker line dividing the colorless sea from the colorless sky. The faithful computer reported the storm was taking its time as it moved across the waters, gaining strength with every mile. She would, however, be safely on the ground long before it could possibly reach into the present latitudes.

The line became a darker mass, which soon resolved itself into grassy downs broken by forested valleys. Her close-up scanner brought into focus small animals browsing in the vegetation, others in the trees, and still others playing at the edge of the sea. As she watched, she became aware that Love was pressed tightly against her arm, his bright eyes fixed on the screen.

She brought the flitter down neatly in a small clearing beneath the knee of a cliff. Sheltered so, she could tie it down to adjacent trees, if there seemed to be any need for that.

Her goal was a couple of kilometers down the shoreline. The telltale would lead her directly to it, when she decided to seek it out. For the time, however, she wanted to stretch her limbs, get some exercise, and see something of this new continent that only the preliminary explorers had touched.

Love scampered down from the flitter and leaped about on the sandy grass at the edge of the water. The playing animals had, of course, gone to cover at the arrival of the strange thing from the sky, but the cavorting Deet seemed not to mind. He climbed a couple of trees, leaped from their tops to the tops of others with acrobatic agility, and ran in circles about Andraia as she bent and stretched, jogged in place, and otherwise loosened her cramped muscles.

When she reached into the storage compartment for the basket of fungus she had brought for him, the creature stopped his play and settled down to eat beside her. She munched dry rations, drank from her canteen, and enjoyed being stationary for a while. When both were done, she rose and looked down the coastline.

"Well, we've wasted as much time as I can square with my conscience," she said to Love. "Better get moving. It will be dark in a few hours, and I want to be back by then."

Love glanced down the beach. He looked up at her appraisingly. Then he climbed her and sat on her shoulder again.

"I see. If you have to go, you refuse to walk, is that it?" she asked. "Well, that's only fair. Your legs are shorter than mine. Here we go!"

She tramped away down the crisp salt grass, with the gentle wash of the ripples keeping her company. This coastline held no sandstone cliff, as did that on her own continent. Rolling hills eased into minor swells as they neared the water, and runoff had cut channels in some of those that left bare soil temptingly vertical.

She was thinking about those dotted symbols

she had found before when Love gave a start and darted down from her shoulder to peer at such a clay bank. His little fingers flew as he punched into the plastic surface the identifying mark she had seen so often.

She went down on her knees to see better, and to her astonishment she found that Love's markings were side by side with another set. This, however, was ["....:..]

Another tribe? She searched along the damp course and found still other sets of the identifying symbols.

"Deet-deet-dit-dit-dit-dah-dit-dit," she said aloud. "If your people are the Deet, these must be the Dit. But that's too close . . . how about the Dah? That suit you?"

But Love was too busy ferreting out other sets of marks, these different from the first. They came in sets. Some of the markings were circles instead of dots, also, which made one set read [.: °..." ::.°..:]
"If that isn't a written language, I'm not standing here," Andraia said to the tiny being beside her. "And you're reading it, or I don't know anything at all."

She rose to stare down at the markings, almost invisible from her position. She took the small camera from her tool belt and knelt again to photograph all the marks she could find, along with Love in the act of reading them by means of both vision and touch.

When she moved on it was reluctantly. She

wanted to see the Dah . . . were they exactly like the Deet? Except for name, of course. And where were they?

But she knew. They were hiding until they could tell whether this huge creature with their distant kinsman might be dangerous.

She didn't blame them a bit.

11

She knew what she would find before she
reached the position of the sensor. And she was
correct: the rodlike device was in place, its button
on the end carefully unscrewed and dropped into the
crack into which it had been set.

Sighing, she took her retrieval wand from her
tool belt and connected its sections. Even as she
climbed to reach the crevice, Love scampered past
her and down into the crack. He popped up, button
in hand, just as she arrived. How had he known what
she intended to do?

Unless, of course, he had been the one who
disassembled the first sensor, back on Continent
One. She stared down at the little person in the
notch. He stared back, eyes bright and quizzical.

Taking both hands for the job, he reached up
and screwed the button back onto the rod. That
sealed it! He knew what the sensor should look like.
He recognized the difference and knew what to do
to correct it. And that was a solid indication that
this was, indeed, a new sort of intelligent being,
nonhumanoid, nontechnological, and nonverbal.

"Welcome to the club," she said softly. "It has

its drawbacks, but perhaps it will keep you and your nice peaceful world from being blasted into rubble."

She checked the button for tightness. It was firm but not as tight as her much larger fingers could make it, and she screwed it fast. Then she jumped down and waited for her companion to join her.

They moved back up the beach, hearing the restless lapping of the water, the sigh of wind that now had shifted to blow from the north. Could that be the first indication that the storm was nearing this area? She hurried her pace, and Love gave up his investigation of a hole in a runnel and came flying to climb onto her shoulder again.

His fingers grasped her ear for balance, and now she detected a pattern in his grip. Pressures from different fingers in recurring sequences—did that indicate communication? In darkness, hand signals would be invisible, of course. Was this the way his kind "talked" in the night?

It was nearing sundown. The sun was hidden behind a sea of spun-glass cloud, showering refracted silver light across the landscape. It was a shadowless illumination, carried by the entire skyful of cloud, that turned sea and land and forest alike into a misty glimmer.

Then, with surprising suddenness, the west disappeared behind an arm of blackness that reached from the north. The sky went to plum color. The sea turned silver-purple. Darkness swallowed everything before she could reach the location of the flitter, and her power-beam seemed to be swallowed up without illuminating anything useful.

As if sensing her bewilderment, Love tugged at her ear. When she obeyed the direction of his pull, she found her feet on level soil. By the inadequate gleam of the power-beam, she saw a familiar shape. A glint of metal . . . the flitter loomed beneath the cliff, sheltered by the buttress of soil and rock, as well as by the big trees on either side.

It was time to batten down. Andraia pulled the cables from their spring-controlled attachments and locked them around trees. She drew out others and pounded pitons into the rock of the cliff. When she was done, a webwork of high-tension cable held the flitter in a cradle of safety—she hoped.

The wind was rising. She could hear the water slashing along the beach on a diagonal course, slapping at rocks, whipping inland to touch her with cold drops that stung her face and hands. She crept beneath the inverted hammock of webbing to take from the cabin of the vehicle her emergency pack, which she dragged into the nearest crevice in the cliff's face, out of the wind.

Love leaped at her, pummeling her with minute fists, tugging her ears, all but scolding her aloud. She shone her light along the floor of the runnel. Runnel? Of course. The runoff from the distant downs would come pounding down this natural guttering system. If there was much rain, she'd be washed out to sea.

"Thank you," she said. Her voice was lost in the roar of wind in trees and the beginning sputter of rain against stone and soil. "But where can I go? I don't want to get blown away!"

The Deet darted away, along the base of the cliff. He returned, looked up at her demandingly, his coat already sleek with wet, and dashed away again. She followed slowly, struggling with her pack as it caught the wind.

The creature turned at last and gestured, an up-and-down motion of his fist. She squatted beside him, and he disappeared magically from sight. As she stared about, a little hand came out of an overhang at her knee's height and tugged at her pants leg.

She went flat and was looking into sparkling eyes. Many of them. She focused the power-beam to peer into the slotlike opening in the rock. It led into a fair-sized chamber that was literally crammed with the people she had called the Dah. They looked uneasy, but there was no sign of open hostility.

Andraia glanced back into rain-slashed darkness. Already her back was soaked. She crawled forward into the rocky cavern and tugged her pack in behind her. Love was standing in the light of the beam, and he was gesticulating furiously.

From time to time one of the Dah would reply with a timid gesture, and the Deet would go into another long discourse. At last he turned to Andraia and set his hand on the lighting device.

Ah. He wanted to turn it upon her . . . to show these people what sort of creature he had brought into their storm shelter. That was natural, as well as the polite thing to do. She unhooked the thing from its flexible attachment and let Love take it.

Even with both hands holding it, the beam

almost fell. Love lowered it to the floor and pivoted it until the light-beam shone directly onto his companion. There came a concerted gasp from dozens of tiny mouths. Faces leaned forward, peering at her until she knew exactly how the alien fauna in the zoological gardens must feel.

Then, seemingly satisfied, Love pushed the beam back to her hand and switched it off, exactly as if he had been used to doing such things for years. There was no light whatsoever. The din from outside was muted but still audible, yet over it, very near her, she could hear many furry bodies moving. Coming toward her.

12

Andraia huddled her knees to her chest, her arms about them. She knew nothing, really, about this tribe of the furred people. Love she trusted, but how could even he be certain of her reception among this group of his people that he could never have seen before? Intelligent as he was, she could not envision his kind building boats to travel across an ocean that must seem endless to them.

A small hand touched her cheek. Then Love crept into her arms and lent his furry warmth to her. She realized that she was shivering with chill. She was wet, and the stone chamber in which she sat was not being warmed by its tenants . . . not yet.

She shook harder still. Her teeth began to chatter, with tension as much as with the cold. Love wriggled from her grasp and was gone . . . there was simply no light by which to see. Then he was back, and she heard again the moving of bodies on stone.

Suddenly she was covered with a fur blanket formed of living bodies. The Dah were cuddling about her, warming her clammy skin, drying with their body heat her sodden clothing. The thought staggered her.

I am an alien! she thought. *How can they*

accept me, help me, without knowing if I am an enemy?

Eased, her teeth no longer chattering, she lay among the Dah and thought very hard. There were no predators on Argent. She had been told that, as well as the "fact" that there were no intelligent beings here. She had discounted that. Never had she studied a world without some sort of large predator. All worlds had birds that ate insects and small animals—the flying creature that she had seen swoop down on small creepers and hoppers proved that to be true here. All had bacteria that digested waste materials, which was also predatory, after a fashion.

What if this was the only world that literally had no enemies for its larger denizens? That would explain the lack of fear when she was revealed to them. It would also explain Love's initial daring in coming to her to ease her pain. Without the concept of enemy, then any creature these people met had to be, by definition, a friend.

She sighed softly, and Love snuggled closer against her throat. She stroked his fur automatically, her mind wrestling with the idea of a world without enemies. Her kind thrived on competition and aggression. Even now, with those attributes controlled and channeled into constructive ways, they were still there.

About her the Dah were vibrating softly. The warmth, the pulsations, the velvety fur reminded her of the hypnocouch. She could even feel her own tensions and emotional problems dimming away to

Suddenly she was covered with a fur blanket formed of living bodies. The Dah were cuddling about her, warming her clammy skin, drying with their body heat her sodden clothing.

nothing under the ministrations of the Dah and of Love. She knew they would return, but what a marvelous thing it would be if troubled people could come here to be healed of all their ills, mental and physical!

Then she had a thought that made her gasp. She was thinking, as usual, from a completely anthropocentric viewpoint. This was the world of the Deet and the Dah and, for all she knew, the Dit and the Doh, which was as near as she could come to finding an appropriate sound for the [○] symbol. They had their own lives, their own purposes, she suspected. Why should they discommode themselves to heal the sick of a species that had nothing to do with them and that had brought most of its own ills upon itself?

"Why should you?" she asked.

They felt the vibration of her speech and vibrated more strongly, more soothingly. She felt every nerve relaxing, and she let the entire train of thought go and sank into sleep.

She woke to see a tenuous light—or perhaps a faint lack of darkness would have been the better term—filtering into the cave. She listened intently, but there came no sound of rain. Instead there was the rush of wind.

The sea was still surging against the shore, as well. She could hear the waves as they flung themselves high onto the salt grass. She hoped devoutly that the flitter was still safe . . . without it she would spend a long time with the Dah . . . only when her weekly "secure" signal didn't come through and a search team was sent would she be found, but that would require months.

Love squirmed in her arms. She loosed him, and he pulled himself free of the piled Dah and shook out his limbs, one by one, stretching and flexing until he seemed satisfied. Then he looked at her in the tenuous light and made his up-and-down fist motion again.

As clearly as if he had been able to speak, he had told her that it was time to be up and doing.

She moved cautiously, not wanting to crush any of the accommodating furred ones as she rolled to all fours, tugged her pack free, and crouched. They moved aside politely. She didn't presume to try stroking any of them as she passed them . . . it seemed to her that it would be taking a liberty.

Once outside the slotlike entrance, she stood and did some stretching of her own. Her muscles had cramped with lying so long in one position, and her feet were almost asleep. Sheltered below the cliff, she and Love were out of the wind, though some spray from the waves found her from time to time.

Once she could walk freely, she followed Love back the way they had come in the storm. The trees to which the flitter was tied came into view as they rounded a gentle curve. The webbing of cable was still in place. She breathed a sigh of relief.

Quickly she checked out the machine. Some of the steel-gray paint had been rubbed away by the restraining cables, but the thing seemed to be intact.

She could return to her Shelter and the Dome and her duties there, one of which, she now knew, would be the close investigation of Love's fellows in the forest.

Love came bouncing up and tugged at her pant leg. He seemed to want her to follow him up the coastline. It was sheltered beneath the cliff, and the waves didn't come very far inland, coming in at a slant as they did, so she went along, hearing the moaning of the wind above her head.

She would begin her serious investigations here, among these remote members of the species. It might be a long time before she could come back for such work.

"Yes, I'm coming," she said, as Love skittered up the wet grass and muddy soil before her. "What in the world do you want?"

After about a kilometer, he paused and pointed (he'd learned that gesture from her on the night she had pointed out the star pattern). Strewn on the grassy beach was a network of cordage.

It was knotted intricately, deliberately, into a webwork the size of a table. At one end, plain as could possibly be, was the signature [.:...]

13

She knelt on the wet ground, taking the network of cord and knot onto her lap. The cordage was
hand-rolled from some sort of flexible bark. She had
seen similar things in museums on some of the
worlds she had visited. The knots were intricate,
some containing loops tied into them.

This was a message from across the ocean. She
knew that, in some unprovable way, and Love's
attitude confirmed it. Were there currents that carried messages back and forth across the waters from
tribe to tribe, keeping them in touch and informed
about their affairs? And what affairs might those be?

Among Andraia's kind it would be news of war,
of business, of technological advances and tremendous projects. What could the Deet and the Dah
have to talk about that would justify such efforts and
such necessarily lengthy spans of time required for
a reply?

She pointed to a flowerlike cluster of knots and
loops. Then she looked hard at Love, hoping he
would understand what she wanted to know and
could find some way in which to convey the information.

He looked hard at her, at the knotted message,

and again at her, as if gauging her ability to understand. Then he pointed at the sky, the sea, and a
nearby tree, whose top extended above the cliff and
was bowed to leeward. He made a circling motion
with both hands, as if tying all three elements together.

A sort of weather report? But why should that
be important enough for such a labor-intensive message? The weather reported would be over and done
with long before the net could possibly reach its
destination. And she wondered how many nets were
made and cast into the sea in order to insure that
one, at least, would make the journey safely.

She beckoned to Love and drew with a handy
rock a pattern in mud. It was the shape of the storm
as showed on her monitor. He had studied it closely.
She thought he would remember it.

He scrubbed out the drawing with a disgusted
movement. He pointed at the sky, and he did a small
dance, bending his flexible body, waving his tiny
hands. He pointed to the sea, and he undulated from
tail to nose in rhythmic motions. He pointed to the
tree, and he quivered, arms extended downwind,
head moving as if agitated. Then he melded all those
motions into something else, evocative and compelling.

Andraia watched, tense with concentration.
She felt the wind moving in her mind. She strained
with the tree, surged with the waves, but there was
another thing as well. She had the sensation of unity
. . . the flowing together of wind and tree and sky
and sea and cloud to form a whole far greater than

He looked hard at her, at the knotted message, and again at her, as if gauging her ability to understand. Then he pointed to the sky, the sea, and a nearby tree, whose top extended above the cliff and was bowed to leeward. He made a circling motion with both hands, as if tying all three elements together.

its parts could add up to. The feel of a storm . . . that was what she had.

The symbol knotted into the network was a metaphor. She understood at last. If each of the many configurations was a metaphor or a mental image or even a feeling, what was the message? A philosophical statement? A question?

Or . . . the thought was staggering . . . a poem?

She rose stiffly. The intricacy of the task before her was almost frightening. She was young at her work. She was not at her best. And this was of great importance, not only to the people of Argent but to the cooperative worlds of all the systems.

If she had found a people without enemies, without technology, who yet lived a creative and active life of the mind, it would be without precedent. It might change the ways in which human beings thought of themselves and of alien peoples.

Why should Man be the master of other kinds? Why should he presume to alter the ways of living, the religions, the very planets of other species?

"We aren't particularly kind or wise or self-controlled," she said to Love, who had climbed again onto her shoulder. "We think only of ourselves, our interests, our short-term goals. We ruined our own world, thousands of years ago. Why should we think we have the right to ruin yours?"

She laid the message-net carefully back onto the grass where Love had found it. Then she turned back down the beach. Her mind was in a turmoil. Everything she had been taught in her training as a xenologist had assumed that she would be, in any contact with alien beings, the wiser, more advanced, controlling factor in the contact.

Why had that been implicit in her training? She thought of the Thryll. If she and Josip had not had the false confidence of that training, would he have been so rash as to agree to participate in that fatal ritual? Might he not have approached those totally unfamiliar people as an inquirer rather than as one who came with every right to explore their lives and habits?

8 1

"We are arrogant," she said to Love. He pulsated against her neck as if agreeing. "We assume that because we behave in certain ways, those are the only proper ways. We have an attitude of superior amusement when we find people whose ways are completely unfamiliar and alien to us. If they were the *right* ways, then they would be like ours." She laughed.

"It is probable, I suspect, that many of the lifestyles and customs of the people contacted by the Service have been far superior to our own, but the officers who made those contacts were constitutionally incapable of recognizing the fact."

She was nearing the flitter again. The wind seemed to be dying down, and the trees above her craft were filled with the Dah, all sitting quietly, staring at the alien vehicle in their midst.

"Now there's a perfect example. My kind would be all over the flitter, if they were in the Dah's shoes. They'd be sawing off pieces of the wings to analyze the metal, prying around inside the cabin to see what was there, taking the computer apart as if they had every right to tear up the property of anyone unlike themselves. But there sit your own people, waiting for permission to come aboard. You tell them to come."

She opened the cargo door of the flitter, through which she could load and unload cases of specimens or equipment. "Come right in, my friends. See the product of nine thousand years of human technology."

It took them only a moment to grasp her invitation. Then, in pairs, they clambered into the flitter, looked about, keeping their hands strictly away from anything that looked complicated, and took their leave.

It made Andraia ashamed of her own kind. People would have pushed and shoved and meddled and asked stupid questions.

It also showed her just how difficult it was going to be to persuade her own superiors, much less the Registrars of Alien Intelligence, that this was a truly intelligent race. She must do her preliminary work with perfect precision. She must draw no unwarranted conclusions, no matter how obvious they might be. Everything must be according to the book.

She laughed. Score one for Alex Fender.

14

When the storm died away, and the silvery ocean was again going about its business in a disciplined fashion, Andraia unfettered the flitter and took it aloft. While she was here, she might as well explore this distant continent. Love, of course, accompanied her. To her surprise, one of the Dah also indicated that he (she? it? The thing was becoming frustrating) wanted to come, too.

This was a larger creature than most of its fellows, and its silvery fur was underlaid with a layer of shorter, plushy fur that had an almost rusty cast. It made him stand out from the rest, particularly when he was in the sunlight. She called him Rusty and welcomed him aboard.

They lifted from the beach into the wind and banked in a curve over the water, moving inland toward the distant downs. Below, Andraia could see lines of trees following the canyons that drained the highlands in forests of mixed conifers and gray-barked softwoods. She went low and made certain that the lower cameras were recording everything she saw.

Among the trees, she realized as she moved along just above the treetops, moved animals. Not animals like the Deet or the Dah . . . these were four-legged, shaped like bovines, though of slenderer build. They lacked the quickness of deer, yet they had a singular grace all their own. As the flitter sighed overhead, they looked up, cocking back square-browed, pointed-nosed heads and showing racks of intricate horns that looped and curled with calligraphic elegance.

Among them were much smaller beasts that looked something like hares and moved like dogs. They too stared up at the flitter without fear. That told her that the predator-birds preyed only on insects and the tiniest of the rodentlike creatures.

No enemies . . . no enemies . . . what a strange concept that was. Rusty was peering down at the creatures below them. From time to time he all but hopped up and down with excitement. His tiny hands kept up a constant chatter of sign language with Love, who also seemed fascinated by the landscape below them.

She lifted and banked again, gaining altitude, as they neared the first of the cliffs that hemmed the high country. An updraft off the grassy plains between the canyons provided an extra push, and she found herself flying over the mesalike terrain, which was covered with pale grass and stunted shrubbery.

It all looked the same as they crossed the first expanse, swung over another canyon, and moved even farther inland. The second of the downs was different. The grass was greener. Shrubs grew in patterns that hinted at cultivation. Patches of heavier growth that showed patches of color seemed to indicate flowering plants or shrubs. The thing was like a gigantic flower garden.

She slipped the flitter lower, staring down at the patterned mosaic of living things below her. Boulders came into focus, placed about with artless effect. The shapes and the placements were obviously artificial.

Love bounced against her shoulder, his hand patting Rusty's furry arm. The Deet pointed downward. Then he nudged Andraia and pointed down again, indicating, she felt sure, that she should go even lower. She obliged, and a group of boulders came into view.

Aligned, the arrangement said: ["..°°°.]

The furry passengers were communicating, their hands flying in intricate patterns. Rusty, in particular, seemed amazed and excited.

"The Doh?" asked Andraia. "I had a premonition they were lurking about someplace."

She banked again to align the flitter with a bare patch of grass and set it down neatly. "Now maybe we can meet this new batch of your people," she said.

She unlatched the hatch and climbed down from the flitter. All around her were low plants that were bright with blossom. The grass was of different sorts, providing a subtle color gradation, and small stones, too little to see from the air, were placed with anxious care to provide changes in texture.

"If your people are poets," she said to Love, "these have to be artists."

The Deet was scurrying about, examining pebbles and plants and shrubs, digging sharp little fingers into the soil and sniffing at them afterward. Rusty was rambling over the gardenlike terrain, stopping now and then to look more closely at a bloom or an individual stone. They seemed almost stunned with surprise, though they showed no sign of wariness.

After a time they came to sit on a flat stone beside her, staring around and resting. While they sat there, a small figure came into view, trundling a pouchlike burden in short arms.

The fur was the same. The basic build of the creature was much like that of her companions, yet Andraia could also see that this member of the Doh had evolved in a slightly different direction. He was shorter of backbone, stockier. The upright stance was more natural to him as he struggled with his armful of container and soil, from which a spray of leaves protruded at the top.

As they watched, he dug a hole at the edge of a patch of silvery-blue flowers and tamped in a small plant, whose pale yellow blooms contrasted nicely with the others in the plot. He stepped back and admired his handiwork.

Andraia was chuckling. She had seen, on many worlds, gardeners at work. This one, for all the differences in outward appearance, was exactly like all the others in basic character, she suspected.

Love went scampering from the stone to touch the gardener on his furred shoulder. He turned slowly, deliberately, to observe the newcomer to his

As they watched, he dug a hole at the edge of a patch of silvery-blue flowers and tamped in a small plant, whose pale yellow blooms contrasted nicely with the others in the plot.

countryside. One hand moved. A question, indubitably.

A flurry of hand motions from Love evoked an enigmatic flutter and flip from this unexcitable character. Love caught his hand and tugged him over to the rock where Andraia was still sitting beside Rusty.

The Doh looked her over. He looked again. He sat on the turf beside the stone and put both hands under his chin meditatively. At last he touched Love lightly on the arm, three deliberate motions of his fingers. Then he was gone around the stone and out of sight.

15

Rusty and Love settled onto the stone as if for a long wait. Andraia followed their example, though she wondered at the Doh's lack of fluency in the hand language. While she waited for him to return, she was thinking hard.

She had been trained not to make unwarranted assumptions. This Doh might be a slow learner among his kind. Yet he didn't quite look like the Deet and the Dah, lacking their svelte quickness. He seemed also to lack the communication skills the other two sorts possessed. He did, however, seem to be visually oriented. It might be an individual quirk, or it might indicate the same attribute in his variety of being. The bright garden demonstrated a love of beauty.

With that thought, she bestirred herself and walked around the gardens, speaking into her computer link, recording with her tiny camera details of the place that could not be seen clearly from the air. When the Doh returned, Love came after her and tugged at the leg of her jumpsuit until she followed him.

Four of the creatures were standing beside the stone, where Rusty was talking rapidly, his hands almost a blur of motion. The faces of these folk were rounder, their bodies podgier than those of their fellows from other places. The expressions on their furred faces were slightly bemused, as if they were entirely unused to such rapid communication.

The largest of them suddenly sat on the ground, as if he were exhausted by the effort of following the hand language of the Dah. His fellows solemnly sat beside him and the four held a short conversation among themselves. Love and Rusty watched their technique as closely as did Andraia herself.

Their hand signals were concise, economical, and probably codified to contain as much information as possible with as little expenditure of energy. A twitch of a finger, the rocking of a palm, the faint ripple of three fingers, the downward motion of a thumb . . . those slight matters replaced the intricate repertory of the others of their kind.

When they were done, they rose to their feet and the big one made what Andraia could only call a speech. The Dah and the Deet watched intently, their own hands twitching, she suspected, with frustration at the slow deliberateness of the other's movements. When he was done, the pair jumped down from the stone and headed for the flitter.

"The audience is over?" she asked their retreating backs. She sighed and looked down again at the solemn four at her feet.

She turned her hand palm upward in the ancient gesture of harmlessness. The big Doh reached a tentative hand to touch her fingers. He tapped her palm deliberately twice. Then he too turned and went away, followed by his companions.

Love and Rusty were waiting for her in the flitter. They had managed to open the hatch, which she had not locked down, and both were sitting in her seat, staring at the instrumentation, watching the flicker of lights in the computer complex, absorbing, she thought, everything they could about her wonderful machine.

So far as she could tell, they had touched nothing.

When she had them settled into their places again, she lifted the flitter to a good altitude and swung over as much of this continent as she thought she could manage before nightfall. It wasn't large—more like a very large island than a continent, actually—and she managed to make a circuit of the entire landmass and return to the beach near Rusty's home by the time the sun was low behind the downs.

She slept that night in the flitter, though Love joined the Dah for the night. She had thought they might return to the cave, but they went up into the trees. The cave was probably just for shelter when there was a storm, she decided.

Alone in the flitter, she reclined the seat and relaxed, listening to the gentle washing of the water. This was such a silent world . . . no hunting animal cried in the darkness. The tree full of intelligent beings just beside her was quiet, though she knew the touch language was probably going at full speed in the branches.

She closed her eyes. She missed Love. His warm fur, his vibrant presence had comforted her for long enough to make her feel desolated when he was not there. *Josip!* she thought, for the first time in many days.

The memory did not devastate her, as it had done for so long. The trauma was moving into the past, as her therapists had told her it would. She felt slightly guilty, as if by allowing it to do that she might be betraying her Link. Then something the hypnocouch had impressed upon her came to mind ... sharply, this time, and in focus.

The dead cannot be betrayed. But the living can betray themselves, their lives and their futures, by yearning after those who are gone.

Now it made sense. Now something inside her was prepared to accept that as true.

"Good-bye, Josip," she said aloud, her voice quiet and sleepy and curiously lacking in sadness. "I will make it now."

She turned on her side, and sleep came like a healing tide to wash over her. For the first time in months, she did not dream.

16

Before the sun had more than cleared the east-
ern horizon, Andraia and Love were aloft, heading
for home. There was much to do, and as she relaxed,
allowing the automatic pilot to control the craft, the
girl was thinking hard about the report she must file
via superlight transmission.

It must be understood as quickly as possible
that this was a world inhabited by intelligent beings.
Plans for weapons testing must be scrubbed at once,
before so much money and prestige had been in-
vested in the project that even her Service would be
hard put to divert the intended devastation.

Her own observations would count for very little, when weighed against the might of the arma-
ment makers and the military complex. She had to
make her report persuasive. Evidence must be offered to support it. She hoped that Alex Fender
wasn't going through one of his periodic paranoid
episodes . . . her report could send him into a tizzy.

She dozed for a time, thought for much longer,
and by the time they set down beside the Dome she
had the gist of her report in hand. The tapes from
the recorders in the flitter would also be edited, the
most valuable parts added to her own words, and the

entire matter zapped off to Base in a burst of incredible energy.

She did not go to work at once, however. It had been a long day and a longer week. She took Love with her into the Shelter. After a balanced meal, dialed from the automatic caterer, she went into the Cleanser and removed the grime of her visit. Sleep was what she needed before tackling the difficult task of making a report that could save a world from destruction.

The next morning found her busy. She edited the many meters of tape carefully, extracting important segments for retaping onto the special material used in the superlight transmitter. Only then did she check her incoming transmission record. Fender might just have come up with the requested materials in the time she had been gone.

There was a ream of routine orders and queries. She read them with amusement . . . why did those in charge of her Service distrust the very people they had put in place?

RECHECK WIND DIRECTIONS SOUTH QUADRANT OCEAN 2, one ordered. As if every ocean on every world must of necessity behave as did those on familiar planets!

SOIL ANALYSIS SHOWS OVERAGE SILICATES. ??? said another. She ran the analyses through the computer again, and the same results showed up. Just the way things are on Argent, she thought. Why can't they accept variations? That's their *business!*

She sighed and sat down to edit the pertinent tapes onto the master for transmission. Her fingers

flew, as the computer devoured the material in sec-
onds and paused for more. This was the toughie. She
sat back, relaxing deliberately.

Love climbed her leg and sat in her lap, pulsating soothingly, and she stroked his fur absently,
staring at the monitor. She was about to upset a
great many applecarts. Her career might well be
forfeit. She could imagine that those with financial
motives might accuse her of mental instability because of her loss of Josip. The problem was on record,
after all. She might end up in detention, editing
unimportant information from robot probes.

She sat up straight, forcing Love to hold to her
tunic with both hands. She keyed the SAVE impulse
and began to write.

5

ARGENT, SECTOR 11837, LATERAL
THREE, DIAGONAL ELEVEN, STARGRID NINE.
Re intelligent life. NOTE: INFORM REGISTRY
OF ALIEN INTELLIGENCE SOONEST.

Report of Andraia Link-Josip(delete)
0423381, dated Terran 11, 706, day 271,
hour 0900.

IMPERATIVE! IMPERATIVE! IMPERATIVE!

Small, gray-furred animals noted Argent by life-probes L–73, L–75, L–79 show
irrefutable signs of intelligence. Translator
useless, as beings are voiceless. Types A
and B (tapes attached and noted) communicate by means of sign language analogous to ancient system devised for use
with deaf on Earth. Nontechnological.

Unable, so far, to determine characteristics of sign language due to lack of ascertainable common ground. Behavior rational, friendly, cooperative. LACK OF PREDATORS ON PLANET PRECLUDES HOSTILE REACTIONS OR WARINESS. Species vulnerable for this reason.

Beginning intensive effort to establish mutual understanding. Former request for information reinforced.

She reread the monitor, checking for flaws. It wasn't perfect, but it would have to do. She touched the TRANSMIT key, and the transmission system twanged like a harpstring. With such instantaneity, the message was on its way. It would reach Fender in just less than thirty-two hours.

She performed her neglected duties about the Dome and the Shelter in an absentminded fashion. Her next task was that of communicating directly, in some sort of mutually comprehensible system of symbols, with Love. The fate of his kind was now in his undersized hands, as well as her own.

She longed with sudden intensity for Josip. He had been the one with an almost empathic ability to interact with alien beings. She had always been the technician of the team. Now she had to recall everything she had ever learned or felt through her Linkage with Josip, trying to acquire at second hand a talent she had not been given at birth.

She wondered suddenly if the Link might work between herself and Love. It did between people.

Between herself and the hypnocouch it worked flaw-
lessly. Could such a chip, connected through nerve
endings on the surface of the little being's skin to
the remnant of the Link still inside her skull, possibly be used to give such dissimilar kinds some sort
of common set of concepts?

Excited by the thought, she put Love into his
pod and retired to the couch. Its programming might
be able to explore the possibilities of such a Linkage.

17

The couch was in a strange mode. Instead of answering her queries as best it could, which was its usual way, the computer began recapitulating the entire history of the Link. While she knew much of the background of the system, she found herself caught up in the tale, some of which she had never thought to explore.

"When the interface between the microcomputer and microsurgery was first discovered in the late twenty-first century, there was much concern expressed as to the morality of using such techniques to teach (program) human beings. The thought of Linking them through such methods was not entertained until decades later, when such scruples were discarded in the stress of the Last Terran War.

"At that time, commanders in the field were Linked to their superiors in strategic headquarters, thus enabling them to allow the strategists and the tacticians to work directly with the actual situation on the battlefield. Shielded by the Damper Field, which disallowed nuclear reactions, ancient battlefield techniques were revived and tested under true battle conditions. The resulting devastation of hu-

man life, territory, and property sickened Man of
war for centuries thereafter, and only with the rise
of power systems in the League of Worlds, three
thousand years later, was war again considered fea-
sible.

"Having worked so well in battle, the Link was
used experimentally among surgeons and their
teams, educators and their students, and psychia-
trists and their patients. In almost every case, the
burden of extraneous emotional content obliterated
any positive result. Only when limited to a one-to-
one relationship was it productive.

"After intensive testing, it was discovered that
if young children were Linked prior to the onset of
puberty their minds grew into a closely knit unity,
amounting almost to a single entity. Such pairs
functioned with augmented efficiency and useful-
ness in many fields, the most unusual of which was
xenology.

"Although this Linkage created pairings that
were completely stable, without jealousy or any of
the stresses caused by lack of communication, it
was not possible to impose it upon the majority of
human beings. Popular opinion held it to be in some
way coercive or immoral. However, those genetically
superior fetuses chosen for crèche nurturing were
matched via computer and Linked at the age of ten,
before being trained for their natural specialties.

"When the Breakdown occurred in the middle
of the twenty-eighth century, it was caused in large
part by the insistence of large portions of the popu-
lation upon retaining antiquated social customs and
moral codes that demanded stress-provoking behav-

ior of those holding onto them. The combination of the augmented understanding of the universe, the human mind and spirit, and the scientific proof of the existence and omnipotence of a Unity analogous to the ancient concept of God shattered rigid sects and social groups whose existence was posited upon their own superiority to anything differing from their positions.

"At this point Society on Earth crumbled into ruin and was only rebuilt after great effort on the part of colonized worlds. When matters were again in order, Linkage was mandatory. Aggression, misunderstanding, and coerciveness declined almost to the vanishing point. War, now, is a matter of cold calculation of advantage, not of emotional/moral outrage.

"The Link has benefited mankind greatly. It is not, however, a perfect solution to interpersonal or interspecies communication. Proceed with caution. Differences can be so severe that communication of them can shatter the receiving mind."

Andraia opened her eyes and sat up. She had been lost in the account until those last words. Now she thought about them. She doubted that anything Love's mind might contain that was derived from this peaceful world would be detrimental to her. The reverse, however, might well hold true. She knew how shallowly buried was her own grief. The traumas inherent in living as a human being would be totally alien to the small Deet.

A limited Link? She put the question to the couch.

"No," it replied. "Even that would probably be

ruinous. This project that you are undertaking cannot be done easily. Put that from your mind. You
will have to work at it with all your mind's power.

"Humankind has become lazy, dependent upon
mechanisms to work and to think and to act. This
is one matter that must be done the hard way.
Andraia Link-Josip, you must detach yourself from
your equipment. You must go and live with the Deet
in his tree. You must make yourself understand his
context and open yourself to his life.

"Communicate, of course, through your computer links. That is your duty and will help you to
prove your point. But do not depend upon anything
except your food supply . . . it is doubtful that the
Deet's fungus would sustain a human metabolism."

Andraia sighed. Then she grinned. Josip would
have loved this!

She rose from the couch and went to stare down
at Love, sleeping soundly in his pod. Could she adapt
so readily to sleeping in a tree?

She went into her quarters and dressed herself
in the toughest jumpsuit she possessed, after don-
ning thermal underclothing that would keep her
warm and dry even in a storm. She packed a selec-
tion of dried foods from the storage locker, along
with a small water purification packet.

She put a first-aid kit into one of the many
pockets of the jumpsuit, along with a pocket knife,
a small power-beam, and a music stimulator the size
of her thumb. She could attach it to her scalp and
listen to melodies she had heard years before, if she
were driven to boredom.

When she could think of nothing else to take that would not automatically care for her, she went into the chamber and bent over the pod.

"Wake up, Love," she said. "We're going to visit your family."

18

Only when Andraia had Love in the forest did the Deet begin to understand what it was that his oversized companion intended to do. She set him into a crotch of one of the silvery-barked trees. Then, putting her foot into a lower one, she climbed up, passed him, and didn't pause until she reached a comfortably flat branch some twelve or fourteen feet above the ground.

When she paused and sat, arranging her small pack and fastening it with straps to the tree trunk, the Deet came charging up the tree trunk, his eyes blazing with excitement. He scurried across her lap, examined her feet, stretched easily along the length of the limb, peered up into her face, and sat on a slightly higher branch, studying her thoughtfully.

She took her notepad from one of her pockets and dotted onto it the symbol of the Deet: [.:...··] Then she set her finger against the dots, looked closely at the Deet, and moved her finger to her chest. "I am a Deet," she hoped she was saying to him.

The wispy tail twitched. The silver eyes widened, and Love's hands clasped before him nervously. Either he had understood her message and was trying to find a tactful way to tell her that she was entirely in error, or he was composing a message of his own.

Instead of doing either, he jerked himself upright, patted the tree trunk emphatically a couple of times, and was gone, darting down the tree so quickly that she lost sight of him before he reached the ground. Andraia sighed and leaned against the curvature of the trunk. Evidently he had gone for reinforcements.

Would she be expelled from the tree? She hoped not, for the couch's recommendation seemed sensible, now that she had thought about it for a while. How else could she come to understand anything of the lives and thoughts of these strange people?

She closed her eyes. The light breeze was whispering through the winter leaves, rustling faintly in the tissue-textured planes. At a distance, she could hear the subtle sound of the ocean as it washed against the salt grass. Undistracted by vision, she could hear, close at hand, a tiny "Zeep! Zeep!" from one of the insect inhabitants of Argent. She suspected that this was the black beetlelike one with silver veinings on his chitinous overcoat.

Relaxing as she had not done even when lying on the hypnocouch, she felt her body make true contact with the wood of the tree. There was the faint throb of life in it, a vibration more subtle than that of the Deet but of the same quality. Pressing her ear against the bark, she heard the many-voiced choir of the leaves as they moved, ruffling against each other and against the tree bark.

She thought of the device in her pocket, meant to provide her with music . . . why should she need it, with such a new and original set of harmonics at her disposal?

She sank more deeply into her surroundings, and beneath the song of the leaves she began to hear/feel the deep-lying throb of the planet itself, conveying itself to her through the roots as they pumped water from beneath the light soil.

She opened her eyes again, fearing to lose what she was hearing, yet wanting to see if she could add to it some visual element. She wanted to see the forest as Love and his fellows saw it.

She was gazing into a pattern of lacework branches, with drifts of the silvery leaves lying like clouds about and between them. The pale gold of the hazy sky lent its gilding to upper surfaces, and the dark mulch of the forest floor was dimly reflected on their lower surfaces.

Color and line and pattern and shading blended into a vision with all the impact of deliberate art. She had seen paintings, on some of her planets of training, that had less aesthetic value.

Somewhere deep inside her, she wondered, *Is art intrinsic in Man, or is it explicit in nature, and our attempts to capture it result in the thing we call our creative impulse?*

A new element was added to the pattern she watched. A silver-furred face peered from behind a branch filled with leaves. Love? No. Another of his kind, she was sure, smaller, lighter of bone, slightly darker in color. She smiled.

Andraia felt as if she were melting, becoming a part of the branch upon which she sat, the tree on which it grew. The silver-gold sunshafts, the mild breeze were all parts of something that was enfolding her, making her its own.

Was this how the Deet felt about their world? Did they move through it as integral parts of its harmonics, feeling themselves to be such? And how had intelligence evolved among them on a world without dangers? She had been taught that such challenges were the stimuli forcing the growth of quick minds. Perhaps it had been so on Earth and those worlds on which her kind had found other sapient species, but she had an intuition that here it was entirely different.

Did the world itself stimulate thought? Did the beauty inherent in all its elements pull from those capable of observing it the capacity to comprehend and to appreciate? Even she was beginning to feel a compulsion, deep as her very self, to learn and to feel and to interpret Argent to her own kind. The thought of its devastation filled her with pain.

Something touched her hand, and she came up through many layers of consciousness to see the smaller Deet observing her anxiously. Had that twinge of pain brought the being to her side? Was pain a disruptive factor in the context of their lives?

She straightened, breaking the contact between herself and the tree. Sitting all about her were Deet . . . some dozen or more of them were waiting patiently until she noticed them. Love was at her feet, his hand familiarly laid upon her boot.

His other hand was explaining something that looked complex to his fellows. When he realized that Andraia was again with them, he paused in his hand speech and darted up her lap to seize the notepad.

He pointed to the symbol she had dotted onto the page. He pointed to her. His hands flew.

Andraia realized that he was asking his people a vital question. She was on trial, here, by a kind that could have no concept of her background or her personality.

She shivered. Then she tucked her feet up and put her chin on her knees. All she could do now was wait. Her mission was up to Love and his furry crew.

19

The Deet moved away through the trees, moving delicately from branch to branch, tree to tree,
their pace deliberate and calm. *The jury will retire
to consider its verdict,* Andraia thought.

Love glanced back at her and flipped his small
hand. She assumed it meant that he'd be back when
he could manage it. She felt that she had, if nothing
else, a friendly advocate.

The light waned slowly, as the sun went behind
the forest and sank below the horizon. The breeze,
which had varied in intensity without quite dying
away altogether, quickened, and she felt its chilly
fingers on her face. She pulled the protective hood of
her jumpsuit over her head and face, leaving only
her eyes exposed. Goggles were added to protect
them, and she fell into a light doze, snug in her light
and easy garments.

She woke once in the night to hear the patter of
rain on the leaves about her as well as on the water-
proof hood. She leaned in a half doze, thinking of
the Deet. Their fur, triple-layered, was wonderful
insulation. In addition, the outermost silver layer
bonded together, when damp, to form a water-repel-
lent mat. Their little hands were tucked away be-

neath their chins, as she had often seen when Love was sleeping. The eyelids were furred, and they had no visible ears. Those wispy tails always curled around their bodies to cover their noses as they slept. They too were well equipped to withstand bad weather in the treetops.

They had no need of constant shelter. Their food came to their hands almost without effort, and, as far as she could determine, the fungus on the branches flourished the year around. The springs running through the forest supplied an abundance of good water, though they seemed to get their needed moisture from the fungi they ate. In such a mild climate, unmotivated by blizzards or starvation or danger, they had found no necessity for creating the sorts of artifacts that early men made . . . to build huts, to plant and reap, or to invent weapons.

The bases of technological society were lacking here. Instead of the mechanistic creations of her own kind, what was it that they did with their intelligence and their energies?

She drifted into sleep again, and the night, the wind, the rain spoke to something deep inside her. For ages beyond counting, her people had shut away the outside world by night or when the weather was threatening. Now she found herself lulled by the motion of the tree beneath her, as well as by the song of the raindrops and the sighing of the leaves. Somewhere in the wood a loose branch suddenly swung free and began tapping a counterpoint to the nightsong.

Andraia woke again, listening. It was the most

sound she had ever heard on Argent, and she was obscurely comforted to know that even here she could find natural noises. The people of the world might be silent, but the world itself spoke in familiar terms. It reminded her of the first night she and Josip had spent on Thryllia.

That had been a world filled with the sounds of insects and creeping animals, of predators and a people whose communication was alien yet audible. The ocean's roar had penetrated far inland, underlying all the rest and tying it into a symphony of sound.

She had not understood that, at the time. Now she knew that something inside her had comprehended and recorded it all. If she should go again to Thryllia—She caught herself up short. The Service would never send her back, even if she asked to go. Yet she knew that this time she would be far better prepared to face the amoeboid people there and understand far more of their strange ways.

Was it the fact of sitting here, unprotected by walls and roof, feeling the being of the planet around her, that gave her this augmented sense of understanding? She wondered, and, wondering, fell deeply asleep again.

When she woke, it was to find herself surrounded by Deet. They sat, as usual, in mannerly order, waiting for her eyes to open. Love was perched again beside her boot, exchanging fluid hand motions with the nearest of his kin. He paused at once when he saw that she was awake.

He climbed into her lap. Burrowing into her

pocket, he found the notepad and pulled it free. He struggled for a bit with her pen, finding it too large for his hands, but at last he touched the right button and the thing became operable.

Laying the pad flat on Andraia's knee, the small Deet painstakingly inscribed onto the erasable plastic page a sequence of dots. [.:...··] He pointed to it. He pointed again toward Andraia.

Every set of hands about her made the same gesture . . . forefinger dipped, fore and second fingers aligned perpendicularly, forefinger dipped twice, fore and little fingers aligned horizontally. Her first lesson in Deet, Andraia recognized.

She repeated the pattern with her own fingers. She lacked the flexibility and finesse demonstrated by the others, but she managed. Whatever the Deet called themselves, she had just mastered the sign language for that name.

She waited for something else to happen, but, as if satisfied with her reply, the rest scampered away into the trees and were lost to her view. Only Love remained beside her, and he was beginning to look impatient.

"Get up from there, you lazybones?" she asked, her tone amused. "Is that what you're telling me?"

She removed the hood and goggles, letting the fresh breeze of morning stir her hair and cool her cheeks. Now she was too warm, and she shed an outer layer of clothing and secured it inside her pack, which she left tied to the tree trunk.

"I hope I can find this tree again tonight," she said to Love.

The Dcct caught her hand and tugged at a finger, pointing downward. She gestured toward the pack and looked inquiring.

He tapped her finger imperatively, looked up at the pack, back at her, down at the ground. He all but shrugged.

"First day at school," she said. "Make way for the new pupil!"

20

The Deet led Andraia away into the wood. He knew by observation, it seemed, that she was entirely too large and awkward to move through the treetops as his kind could do.

Their direction was southward and east, away from the dim susurrus of the ocean. The forest grew thicker, more enveloping as they went, and the sky disappeared beyond a lacework of pale branches and winter leaves, with here and there a conifer intruding its dark crown into the lighter growth.

The light grew dim, though she could tell through occasional rifts in the overhanging foliage that the sun still shone with silver-gilt luster. But now the forest was so dense that she had to stoop to go beneath thrusting branches, sidle between the boles of young trees whose crowns were a hundred feet above her, fighting for light with their older fellows. The thick padding of old leaves beneath her feet smothered the sounds she might have made, and Love's small feet didn't even rustle as they moved over the mulch.

They came through a tangle of branches that seemed locked into unending combat for the limited space available to them. They found themselves in a clearing centered by a group of trees from which the climbing vines and the extra growth had been pruned.

The upper ranges of the trees, all conifers, were alive with silver-furred shapes. This was, she realized, a "city" of the Deet, sheltered from the winds by the thick forest and from the rain by the canopy of needles. There were all sorts and sizes of that people, she saw as she came closer.

She had wondered, before, that there seemed to be no young among those she had seen, and now it was evident that those more vulnerable ones did not leave this safe and weather-resistant spot until they were old enough to survive the more exposed life in the thin forests nearer the coast.

Love led her to a spot between two of the thick boles and motioned for her to sit. She dropped onto the dampish needles there, relieved at the chance to rest. Working her way through the thickness of the wood had been hot work, as well as tiring. As she panted, wiping her hot forehead, a very small Deet approached Love and caught at his hand.

There was a rapid exchange of sign language. Then Love led the youngster toward her and let it climb onto her boot. She went very still, hoping not to frighten the child, but she need not have feared. It moved up her boot, the leg of her jumpsuit, and touched her hand. It was this fearlessness that bewildered her, she saw. Used as she was to worlds full of peril, beings with good reason to be fearful, she could not accustom herself to one where there was no context in which fear could be formed.

She extended her finger, and the little Deet clung to it with both hands as she lifted him to sit on her shoulder. It quivered with delight. Andraia became aware that another Deet had come from behind the tree on her left to watch the proceedings carefully.

The mother of this precocious youngster? It would make sense, although she had not been able to find sexual apparatus on Love. She had not, however, turned him up like a kitten to make certain— you just didn't do that with another intelligent species, no matter how curious you might be.

Now the newcomer came near to stand beside Love. This one was slightly larger than her old friend, somewhat lighter in shade, and had an odd bulge riding between chest and abdomen. Andraia watched breathlessly as the female (it had to be!) reached into a fold of skin and drew forth an infant not much larger than the human woman's smallest finger.

"Marsupials? Or something very similar," she said aloud.

The Deet held the tiny ball of fur high, so it could see its sibling clambering over this living mountain. Love was talking furiously, evidently explaining to the female the story of his discovery of such a strange being on their world and in their forest. Andraia wanted to laugh. It had to sound like a tall tale to this skeptical-looking Deet, but she couldn't deny the evidence of her eyes.

She came at last, following Love rather reluctantly, to meet his new friend. Were they mates?

Andraia couldn't be certain that in this culture the term meant anything at all. But they were engaged in some sort of relationship, that was certain.

The Deet, with their usual exquisite courtesy, had remained in their trees, busy about their inscrutable duties, while this had taken place. Now Love tugged at her pants leg again, and Andraia rose. He gestured up the tree.

She looked up . . . and up. It was a long way, even to the first layer of branches, but layers of dead growth had been broken off below, leaving stubs. Removing her boots, she set her chilly feet onto the rough ladder and went up to meet her intelligent species at home.

The branch onto which Love led her was wide— at least a meter and perhaps a bit more. Strands of silvery fur caught in the bark, which was worn practically smooth in the center of the limb, indicated that this was occupied frequently.

She looked up again. Above her was a flat plane of thick-needled branches, capable of filtering out any but the worst downpour. Against the trunk there was space for a number of adults and any number of children to shelter, if the weather should turn foul. Enclosed in their efficient fur, the tiniest wrapped yet again in their mothers' pouches, they could endure any sort of weather the world might throw at them.

Could she? The storms had been coming at about five-day intervals, sweeping in from the northwest as they were pulled by the jet streams down from the ice cap at the top of Argent. If she remained

Removing her boots, she set her chilly feet onto the rough ladder and went up to meet her intelligent species at home.

with the Deet for several days, she would probably learn just how they rode out those tempests.

She knew that she would need her outer clothing . . . how could she indicate that to Love? After bringing her so far, he would probably be reluctant to go back after the pack she had left in the treetop. She didn't want, however, to end up with pneumonia.

She crossed her legs on the branch and touched Love's shoulder. She pulled up the leg of the jumpsuit, showing the bare skin beneath it. She shivered dramatically and pointed to the darkening canopy of branches.

Love was quick-witted. A burst of hand signals sent four of his companions dashing away through the treetops.

21

The next four days were fascinating. Most of the time Andraia sat in the top of one or another of the main trees, watching intently, speaking into her com-link, taping the activities of the Deet as they went about their daily routines. The small people paid little attention to her unless she specifically indicated that she wanted to communicate with them.

Thus it was that she saw a Deet female give birth to three infinitesimal youngsters that immediately moved into her pouch. The terrestrial opossum, Andraia recalled, had similar procreative methods. The female, once the young were settled, groomed herself tidily and returned to picking long strands of bark from the tree branches.

She pulled them between her tiny hands, arranging them just so. Then she rolled them between hands and the bare sole of one small foot, forming a smooth length of cordage, to which she added material at intervals. Andraia realized that the cord could be made any length necessary. This was the source, or one source, of the lacework "message" she had seen on that distant beach.

She followed the Deet's progress, as she made a

dozen cords of the same length, some four meters, and took them down the tree to hang them over a low branch near a huddle of her kind. These were sitting flat on the ground, knotting the cords intricately. One of the workers knotted each individual cord along its length, putting groups of the knots in precise patterns.

Another linked cords that had already been individually knotted into a mesh, each connecting knot being of a different kind. The third created the rosettelike bunches of loops at selected intersections, and when Andraia looked closely she could see that each rosette was different from all the others.

Each of the workers would, from time to time, rise from his or her task, wander into the space between the tree trunks, and perform a sort of dance, swaying, rising onto minuscule toes, spinning, bending low to sweep hands above the ground. Each dance too was different. She found that each dancer evoked a different emotion with his motions.

When the dance was done, the small dancer would return to work, fingers knotting even more quickly, its entire body seemingly devoted to the task of creating the cord message. Andraia taped the entire sequence over several days, thinking intensely about the significance of what she was seeing, all the while.

It was the only cooperative effort she saw the Deet make. There was no need for building, for food gathering, or for hunting or war. Those were matters for the peoples of less fortunate worlds. The others of the Deet ranged through the forest, found their own food, enjoyed, she suspected, the ever-changing arrangements of trees and sky and light and shadow.

On the fourth day, Love came to her and gestured toward the sky. He tugged her up the tree in which she had stowed her pack, once the four couriers had brought it, and pointed imperatively toward it. He stared upward again, and her gaze followed his. A bank of dark cloud was covering the patch of sky visible from their clearing.

The storm was coming, right on schedule, and Love wanted her inside her own "fur," protected from the chilly wind. She grinned and pulled on the extra layer, laying the hood back until she needed it.

She thought that the Deet would probably begin huddling against the tree trunks, sheltered by the overhanging branches. When they began climbing high into the trees, to the limper tips of the conifers, she wondered what they could possibly be doing. They would catch the full force of the wind, added to the whip of the bending boles. A really big blow could send them sailing across the wood to break their small bones against other trees.

When he was satisfied that she was fully clothed against the storm, Love tugged again, indicating that she should climb with him to the top of the sturdy tree in which they sat. She could see that the normally placid little person was excited, almost exhilarated, in fact. He took her up and up until the girth of the trunk was too slender for her further progress.

Regretfully, he left her there and continued

climbing until he had reached a ridiculously slight area near the top. Already, the forest was beginning to sway and curtsy in gusts that came rushing from the northwest. The treetops filled with Deet were bouncing, and the small figures, arms wrapped tightly about their perches, were riding the gusts, their attitudes expressing as much as hand language could ever have done . . . sheer pleasure shone from their silvery coats.

Andraia had a sudden intuition . . . was this the only danger they ever knew? Did they, every few days, put themselves at risk in the treetops, when the storms came?

She took a length of cord from a pocket and strapped herself tightly to the tree trunk. It was probably a compliment, Love's invitation for her to share this experience with his people. This might well be the equivalent of a religious experience for the Deet.

Why had not the Dah, beyond the ocean, done something similar? They had huddled in their cavern, out of the wind, safe and dry. But she knew too little to make a judgment. Perhaps those people, so near the ocean, played mad games with tides and currents and waves.

But there were no tides . . . she sighed. It was hard to get used to the habitual sameness of Argent. Without the storms, it would be a very dull place.

And there, she suddenly realized, might be her answer. The Deet were intelligent. They relished the occasional tumult of the storms. Danger, it might well be, was a necessity for every intelligent kind, whether it be natural or intentionally courted.

The tree beneath her swayed deeply toward the southeast. Her breath caught in her throat. Never had she felt such exhilaration, such fierce pleasure.

The needled branches sang shrilly about her. The wind roared across the forest and caught the tree again, sending it even more deeply into another curtsy. Andraia's hair streamed about her face, tangled with the whipping branches, caught a crop of needles and winter leaves, brought from the forest's floor.

Heart pounding, she rode the bucking treetop, while around her ecstatic Deet savored the conquering wind.

22

The Shelter seemed entirely too safe, too con-
fining, too removed from the body of the world when
she returned to it. Andraia had lived, in the week
she had spent with the Deet, more intensely than
ever before in her technology-oriented life. How, she
wondered, did Love bear living with her?

Sitting at her console in the Dome, she edited
onto a Master all the tape she had made during her
stay in the forest. Her commentary from the com-
link was dubbed into the material at appropriate
intervals, but the time in the treetop amid the storm
was orchestrated solely by the roar of wind, the hiss
and shriek of gusts amid needles, the inadvertent
gasps from her own throat.

As she worked, she lived again that fantastic
experience. She had seemed at once a part of the
sky, of the earth, and of the forest. The tree trunk
she rode became a part of her flesh, rough and
familiar against her hands. The motions of her own
tree and those about it were a wild ballet of movement, and her glimpses of the small bundles of
soaked silver fur told her that the Deet seemed as
enthralled as she was herself.

Her eyes streamed tears, both from the chill of

the wind and the impact of the hurtling raindrops. She blinked often, but she didn't shield her face behind the tree. The rush of the air against her face, the wild streaming of her short hair, the breath-snatching wonder of the experience were all too valuable to waste.

As she watched, the tip of a nearby conifer snapped off. The Deet clinging to the upper portion made no sound as it clung to the failing support. A tough strand of bark held it for a few minutes, while the wind shipped the needled clump against the parent trunk. Then it fell free, and the small one disappeared with it into the rain.

She had felt sick with pity. Yet she had known, with some intuitive certainty, that the small one would have chosen that end, given the opportunity. It *had* chosen it. This was the sole danger the Deet could find on all their placid world. She would not have denied them that stringent pleasure if she could.

Now, safe in her chair, she felt again the intense, painful pleasure she had known in her treetop. She could never, she knew, put into any report a trace of that experience. Emotion was suspect among her kind, and emotion in one with a history of psychological disturbance, no matter how it had been caused, would persuade her superiors of her instability.

She watched the tape of the creation of the coded lacework. If that didn't convince the Registry, nothing would. The close-up of the twisting of the cord showed the careful and skillful handiwork of the small female at its best.

Her first ftl transmission had gone out a week before . . . surely Fender had received it by now and could be sending the information she had asked for at any time. Even if he had had to consult his superiors, search through obscure computer sources, even get the approval of the Registry and the Service Committee, he should be coming through with it soon.

Even as she sent the transmission of this new material on its way, the receptor began to beep. The molecular alterations in the recording discs were receiving the incoming message, and she moved on oiled casters across the space between the transmission console and the receptor.

It took ten minutes to finish the recording. Andraia waited impatiently as the sign-off signal came through. She took the paper-thin disc from the mechanism and slipped it into its permanent housing in the readout. When she touched the key that activated that, she gasped and sat straight.

The first line of words on the monitor said: KILL ONE ALIEN CREATURE. NOTE REACTIONS OF SINGLE SPECIMEN, ACTIONS OF GROUP. INTRODUCE DANGER INTO HABITAT AS EXPERIMENTAL METHOD OF ASSESS-MENT.

"Like hell I will!" she said aloud. "Has Fender lost his everlasting mind?"

She read the rest of the reply with increasing unease. Fender had not, as she had requested, notified the Registry. He had consulted with someone in the hierarchy of the Service, and he did not name that officer. The material on communication with the blind and the deaf was there, to some extent, but she had the distinct feeling that it was not anything that would give her any help in communicating with the Deet.

The receptor beeped again. Another message? That was unheard of, except in wartime conditions.

This disc was even more disturbing than the first. Evidently, some higher authority, yet, had been brought into the situation.

> FORMER ORDER COUNTERMANDED. MAKE NO
> FURTHER EFFORT COMMUNICATION ANIMALS
> ARGENT. DO NOT, REPEAT DO NOT LEAVE
> DOME AREA. DO NOT, REPEAT, DO NOT CON-
> TACT ALIEN ANIMALS. READY EQUIPMENT FOR
> CHANGE OF CARETAKER.
> SHIP WILL CALL SOONEST. PREPARE FOR DE-
> PARTURE.
>
> FENDER.

But it was not Fender's style. Someone whose interests were not aimed toward the welfare of the Deet was in command of Base, it was evident. She had no intention of obeying his, her, or its orders, no matter what the result might be.

As for leaving Argent at this point . . . she chuckled. No one knew better than she that it would take at least six months to target a ship to her remote position. In the meantime . . . she had a sudden thought that turned her cold. Would they . . . could they possibly decide . . . to shut her down via remote?

She had seen one such case: a primitive people

had killed the xenologists on site and seized the equipment and the Dome and Shelter. Such a contingency had been provided for, and the ftl signal had deactivated all the automatic processes, frozen the flitter, and shut off all outgoing transmissions from on-planet.

If they should decide to do that in this case, there would be no way in which the message about the Deet could be sent directly to the Registry. Someone at Base, she began to fear, had a vested interest in the predetermined use for Argent and did not intend to see the project changed.

Her hands flew over her keyboard, setting in the Emergency Shutdown Code. As each segment was coded, she knew that access to Argent decreased, and when the last was in place no incoming transmission of any sort could reach her equipment. Even as her monitor assured her that the shielding was up, a blur of light touched the screen.

She sighed, heart pounding. By the fraction of a second she had prevented herself from being immobilized, for that scarlet blip had been the signal of incoming FREEZE, via the ftl system. She'd beaten them, so far. But what next?

23

Andraia felt drained. She had avoided catastro- phe by such a tiny margin that it left her limp to think of it. This would not be the first time, or regrettably the last, that someone—or more than someone—in the Service had disregarded a clear and present duty in order to pursue some personal goal or profit.

There was one other thing they might do. When they realized that she had not responded to the transmissions from Fender, which would take place in just under thirty-two hours, they might well understand her position. Would they send along the path of the signals one of the weapons devised for dealing with intransigent locals? Such a bomb, tiny though it was, could wipe every trace of her and her equipment out of the small valley in which she sat. That would effectively prevent her from informing the Registry of her find.

She turned to her console again and retrieved the now-useless message that had just been sent to Fender from the computer's memory. She worked for an hour at compressing all the vital information into the briefest possible format. Only the most important of the tapes of Deet, Dah, and Doh life and habits could be included in this last emergency signal.

When she was satisfied, she retrieved the tiny coil of tape that was the only method for sending this sort of message. Every Station, on whatever world it might be located, was equipped with the facilities for sending off one life-or-death message at speeds less than the ftl, yet much faster than normal transmission. To use it for the purpose she intended was probably totally illegal. Only to send a last vital message before dying in some mortal emergency justified its use.

She wound the tape onto the spindle and clipped on the cover that should protect it from anything from solar radiation to a landing in a volcano. The spindle fitted exactly into the torpedo shape of the carrier.

This was a miniature spaceship whose drive, unimpeded by cargo or passengers or any particular bulk of its own, could send it whipping across the parsecs, stitching itself through the various warps of space-time involved in moving from one galaxy to another, in incredibly brief periods of time. Given any luck at all, by the time a ship could make planetfall in orbit about Argent, ready to remove her from her station, her message would be in the hands of the Registry of Alien Intelligence.

That was the one organization she had ever known of that had no record of malfeasance. Only the best people, educators, anthropologists, biologists, theoretical physicists, were ever named to that illustrious group, and they took their responsibili-

ties seriously. Not one of them was open to financial
or moral pressure that might make them look the
other way as some backward but undisputably intelligent species was misused or eliminated.

Andraia, Love at her heels, left the Dome and
went to the launcher, placed there just for such a
contingency as she now faced . . . life or death. This
time it was not her life or death that was in question—or she hoped as much—but those of the people
of Argent. As she shot the tube into the launcher
and set the switches to ignite the minute amount of
fuel, she felt her whole body clench like a fist. So
much rode with this small artifact!

She retreated to the Dome, touched the key
that activated those switches. On her monitor, she
watched the brilliant streak that marked the depar-
ture of the shiplet. Love, beside her, touched her
cheek questioningly, and she stroked his fur absently. If only she could explain to him the issues
that were at stake here.

She sighed. On Shutdown, there was no need to
tend the Dome. No messages would come or go until
some sort of resolution was reached. Until that time,
she had an urgent feeling that it would be well for
her to leave the area of Dome and Shelter before
someone back at the Base could think of obliterating
her uncomfortable presence, together with all her
evidence.

Where could she go? Love's people were too
near. The position of the Dah and the Doh had been
recorded and sent with her last transmission. She
needed to find a position that she had not visited,

had not mentioned in any report as being interesting. She needed the flitter to find such a place. She would have to use the land-crawler to move what equipment and supplies she might need, once that was done.

She stood and looked around the Dome. She would not need any heavy-duty com-equipment. The devices for analysis and assessment were, at the moment, useless to her. She would take the light computer, with monitor and link to the mainframe. Even that small mechanism could store far more data than she was likely to need, if the mainframe should meet with any . . . accident.

The light recorder. The small laser, with attachments for drilling, cutting, or use as a weapon. She itemized, as she looked around her. Not too much for the crawler to carry easily. She would need the water adjusting system from the Shelter, for most of the water on Argent, pure and sparkling as it looked, harbored microorganisms that her intestinal flora couldn't handle.

The supplies of freeze-dried foods from the automatic caterer . . . she foresaw a long time of eating tasteless food, for she was a most indifferent cook. Enough polyply to form a shelter, a groundsheet, and extra material for patching, if one of the storms should damage what she had built.

She knew that the weather-resistant layers of clothing could be cleaned simply by turning them inside out and letting them flap in the wind . . . that was no problem. But summer would come before she was done with her camping out. She would also need lighter clothing. That wasn't a problem, either.

Tools. She had forgotten tools, used as she was to mechanisms that did almost everything needful automatically. She would now have to try her hand at using a hammer, a manual cutter, a heat sealer. Perhaps she might even try something esoteric, like scissors or a spade.

She felt excitement building in her. This was adventure . . . she found that she had always longed for something of the sort. Since losing Josip, that longing had been lost amid her own grief, but now it surged up again.

"I am about to meet nature hand to hand," she said to Love.

The Deet looked up at her, its small eyes bright and knowing. He couldn't hear, but she was beginning to believe in his empathic sense. It was not only pain that spoke to him. Excitement and joy also got through to him.

24

The flitter rose lightly from the grass, and Andraia turned its nose inland. She had explored along
the coast, for that was where most of the sensors
had been placed by the preliminary exploration
crew. She had crossed the ocean. What she had not
done was go farther inland than a few hundred
klicks.

Now she settled into her seat, chose an altitude
high enough to avoid up and down drafts yet low
enough to allow her to observe visually as well as
through the sensors in the belly of the flitter, and
pushed the speed controller to medium-high.

Love, in his usual spot beside her, wriggled a
bit until the motion soothed him. Once he slept,
she was alone with her observations and her sometimes unwelcome thoughts. She had cut herself off,
probably irrevocably, from her own kind. Her fate,
whether she stayed on Argent or went elsewhere,
was now tied to that of the silver-furred people.
Searching her memories, she tried to find some
vitally important contribution such a passive people
might make to the sum total of intelligent life.

They had no technology that any of her peers
would recognize as worthy of the name. They

couldn't speak. They had little or no social organization and no elected leaders that she had been able
to determine. Yet they lived actively, interestingly,
and they did things that had importance to themselves, if to no one else.

The one thing she had seen that might impress
anyone, from the Service people to the Registry, was
that knotted message that had been entrusted to the
ocean. She must take with her, if Love consented to
accompany her in her exile, a great deal of cordage.
That would save the time expended in making it
from tree bark.

The forest was a silvery blur below, with occasional glades whose grasses had been tinted pale
golden by the frosts of winter. Across them, from
time to time, moved more of the horned animals
she had seen beyond the ocean. These seemed to be
a bit smaller, slenderer, and faster than their coun-
terparts, yet they were unmistakably the same species.

Why were there no predators to keep their numbers under control? She punched up figures on the
usage of the grasslands she had flown over that
morning. It was abundant and thick, with no detect-
able signs of overgrazing. She saw no herd of more
than eight or ten individual animals, and of that
number no more than two would be young ones
without horns, or infants.

The Deet, with all their intelligence, the safety
of their environment, and the abundance of food
supply, were also limited in number, with few infants in any group she had yet encountered. Was it
possible that on this world, alone of all she knew or

had studied, its tenants exercised control of their numbers? And why? That question would, she knew, fascinate and frustrate anyone sent to study Argent, as a result of her insubordination.

Ahead, she could see a sawtooth line of peaks. Mountains . . . she had been told that they existed on this world, though they were modest ranges, without the drama and excitement of those on most other planets. The dim plum-purple line became more distinct as she drew nearer. As she came over the foothills, she saw that long valleys cut between the eminences, the grass sheltered there still touched with green.

Something skittered beneath her flitter, hopping like crickets over the pastureland. Not the hornbeasts. These were leggy creatures with tiny bodies, long necks. She zoomed a close-up on her monitor and looked into a terrified tan face, whose dished nose and popped eyes gave it a comical appearance. It dived into a clump of grass and disappeared as she watched it.

Nowhere, as she lifted to cross the first line of mountains, could she see signs of overgrazing, or erosion, or of any other abuse of the terrain by overpopulation. She banked around a gentle peak and found herself staring down . . . and down . . . and down . . . into a deep valley whose bottom glinted with a thread of shining river. The unobtrusive mountains on the surrounding sides all but hid it from any except a direct fly-over, and she did not wonder that it had not shown up on the scan she had been given.

She felt out the air currents and gentled the

143

flitter down above the river, finding that what she had thought was emerald-green grass was actually thick forest. Hardwood, she thought, of a kind she had not seen elsewhere. She found a grassy span beside the water and landed, setting the craft straight down onto a smooth spot.

It was silent. Only a rustle of falling water, so distant as to be almost inaudible, came to her ears, for there was no wind. Not even a breeze stirred the leaves, which were summerlike in density and color. The trees were tremendous. Only vines crept from the floor of the forest into their crowns. Deep mulch of thousands of years of discarded leaves lay beneath them. She could set up her shelter beneath the trees, use the water from the river in her purifying system. She could not be found, even by the body-heat detectors, with so many life-forms populating the area.

She walked into the forest, staring up into the treetops. After a time, she realized that she was being observed, as well.

Love, who had lingered in the glade, came scuttering after her, his eyes wide as he observed what had to be unfamiliar terrain. Suddenly, he ran up a tree, hands and feet finding all but invisible holds, and disappeared into the foliage.

She waited patiently, finding a place to sit on a gnarled root. He would return when he was ready. The Deet did what seemed good to them. The fact that it had also turned out to be beneficial to her didn't give her any illusions about being able to command the small people.

25

Andraia was glad she had brought camping supplies, for it was a long time before Love showed
himself again. The sun was behind the mountains,
and she had risen from her root and returned to the
flitter, removing a shelter and poles, her sleeping
bag, and enough dried stuff for a light supper before
he scampered into view.

She had her cooker hooked up to the flitter's
storage batteries, heating the mess of dried fruit and
meat and vegetables she had mixed, when he appeared. The Deet sniffed deeply, looked disgusted,
and dived into the flitter after the store of fungus
she always brought for him on their travels. When
he was satisfied, he waited patiently until she had
eaten.

She cleaned the container and folded it into its
holder, unhooked the leads, put away the microwave
cooker in its box. By the time she was done, the sun
was down, and Love was all but dancing about her
feet. His impatience had him all over her before she
realized that he had some project of his own afoot.

"All right, what is it? You want me to go?" She
pointed toward the trees, then at herself. Love

dashed away, trusting her to follow at her slower pace.

Light, reflected from the height to their east and from the pinkish sky of sunset, allowed her to keep track as she hurried after him. He scurried to the foot of one of the largest of the trees and looked upward, his shape almost invisible against the silvery bark of the tree trunk.

Before she reached him, another furry figure joined him, and another. By the time she came to a stop, very near the line of Deet (or possibly four Ditto and a Deet), they were sitting neatly together, facing toward her, their eyes bright in the twilight.

"I am a very *young* xenologist," she said to the waiting aliens. "But maybe that is a good thing."

She sat on the ground, amid a scurf of dead leaves and twigs, and pointed to Love. She took a bit of twig and dotted into the loose stuff: [.:...·] Then she pointed again.

She handed the twig to the nearest of the strangers and pointed to her symbol and to Love yet again. The creature looked interested, as nearly as she could determine. It fiddled with the twig for a moment, while making signals with its free hand.

There came a flurry of motion in reply. Decisively, the small being began making marks onto the ground. [...··:...]

"I was right. You are the Ditto. Every one of you has its own symbol for your own tribe, I suspect." She thought hard for a moment. She took another twig and wrote into the mulch: ANDRAIA. Then she touched the twig to her own face. Again she went through the ritual. And at last she handed that twig to the alien.

The group had watched her with rapt attention. The Ditto was reaching for the twig before she had it fully extended. Though the light was almost gone, she could see the pale dust of the soil as it was exposed by the scratching of the Ditto. [.../.] He handed the scrap of wood to the next in line, and that one made his own symbol: [...|^]

Each of the four had his own "name." Love, intrigued by this new activity, took the twig in his own turn and for the first time she saw his own name for himself: [.:-]

She had learned something valuable. The individual names of each of these people began with the initial symbols for the tribal designation. Also, while the knotted message was entirely done in dots and clusters of rosettes, the written language could use straight and even broken lines. This hinted at a flexibility that she had not suspected.

She nodded to each of the small ones, though now it was almost too dark even to see motion. "I am happy to meet you," she said. She rose to her feet. "I hope to see you tomorrow!"

As she turned back toward her shelter, she heard the faint scuffle of Love's small feet in the leaves behind her. She was grateful for his company, but it wouldn't have astonished her if he had chosen to sit all night in a tree, communicating with these new-found kinsmen.

She found it hard to sleep. Not because of the emotional trauma that had troubled her for so long—that seemed to be lost in the rush of new problems and emergencies she now faced—but because she needed to find some way in which to warn these innocents of the danger that hung over their furry heads.

Even as she mused upon the matter, she found herself wondering why, among all the worlds, many of them barren and uninhabited even by so much as a microbe, this had been chosen as a test site. Unless—she sat upright in the darkness of the silent night—there were weapons that someone wanted to test on living creatures, which was becoming less and less acceptable among the League of Worlds.

There were many sorts of living creatures on Argent. She tallied those the computer had shown to her when she studied her new assignment: Air-breathing mammals, not unlike earthly whales, in the oceans. Furred creatures of all kinds, both ruminants and others. Several sorts of true fishes. The predator birds. Large horned beasts (which she had now seen for herself) of a kind nearly identical with Terran Cervidae.

Eleven thousand kinds of animals had been noted on the entire world. Weapons used here would be tested for a wide spectrum of effects on living creatures. Could someone be toying with the notion of reintroducing radiation weapons into the military armaments?

Andraia shuddered. That had been prevented, on Earth, by the Damper Field. But who, among all the worlds now active in the league, still remembered how to build such a field? Not a single world that she had ever heard about had ever considered building the device that generated it. That was a matter of historical interest only.

Surely there was no one in her own Service who was so warped as to bring from their long inactivity the brutal weapons that had devastated the ancestors of the human breed? She lay back, curled tightly about herself, and pulled the bag about her head. She had never been afraid . . . not even on Thryllia when Josip had died. Her trauma was that of loss, not of fear.

Yet now, safe in this hidden valley on this remote world, she shivered with terror. Death was not a matter for such quaking. It was not a thing she feared or would fear ever again . . . she had already died, Linked with Josip, and it was the pain preceding that final peace that had been devastating. What shook her to her bones was the thought that someone who was trusted by everyone in the Service was possibly a traitor to the hard-won civilization her kind had found at last.

26

Morning found her busy. She locked into her flitter's navigational system the exact location of the valley. She placed her shelter amid the trees, invisible from the air, and only then did she indicate to Love that they must leave.

His small hands flew, and it taxed her hard-won knowledge of the sign language to understand him.

"Not go!" was his protest. "Good people here. Much learn here!"

She moved her own hands in reply. "We must go. There is something that I must do. We will come back, when we can. Now we must go to the place near your own people." She hoped he understood at least some of it.

Love was always ready for a new adventure, however, and he tucked himself into the flitter at last. Andraia took off, to bank above the river, surveying the valley closely. She could study tapes of this small system, once she was established in this new location. When she had gained altitude and cleared the mountaintops, she found herself wondering if she would find her Shelter still intact. She shook herself and straightened in her seat. It was too soon. The officials waiting at Base for her reply to their last order would not know for a day, yet, that she had not replied. And their signal to destruct, sent even in the speediest way, would be more days in returning. She had plenty of time to make herself and her equipment safe.

She came back to the familiar clearing in late afternoon. The Dome was shining dimly against the pale grass, and the Shelter squatted, almost invisible from the air, beside it. She put the flitter down neatly and climbed from the cockpit, stretching her cramped limbs as she stood beside it.

Love joined her there, and her mood of nostalgia seemed to affect him. He was very quiet as they entered the Shelter for food and a cleanup. Only when she had revived herself somewhat and moved to the Dome did he liven up. He watched with interest as she collapsed the heavier stuff into its shipping modes and trundled it away from the immediate area of the Dome on the crawler. She found an overhang beneath a bluff, under which she stowed the valuable things from the workshop/com area. The ground sloped down from that; any rainfall would run away rather than toward, the spot.

She had intended to take some of that bulky equipment with her on the crawler, but the distance to her perfect hideaway was too great for her to use that slow vehicle. Only the lightest stuff would go with her into exile.

She knew, of course, that there was time to do the task by day, yet she was obscurely uneasy. Even if she had gone to bed, she would not have been able to sleep, so she worked the night away, using the powerful light sources of the crawler to make her way through the forest, back and forth. When the last of the most useful of the equipment had been stored, and the entire pile had been covered tightly with weatherproof film, she found herself with a small heap of materials that would go with her in the flitter.

The computer, of course, with monitor and a flat pack of the discs that held in permanent storage the information transferred to them from her scanner and personal tapes, would go. In addition, she had packed many discs showing the arts, the history, and the activities of her own kind. The Deet and the Ditto would understand, she felt certain, the things they could see with their own eyes.

The hypnocouch would stay behind—it was simply too bulky to carry, even in its compact form. Yet she had the feeling that she would not need it, now. Faced with a problem concerned with the real world and immediate danger, she found those psychological and emotional upheavals had begun to seem like self-indulgence.

She slept, when she went to rest at last, like one dead. Love curled beside her on her couch, his vibrations soothing her weary muscles and troubled mind.

She rose at mid-afternoon and loaded the rest of the supplies onto the flitter, removing it to an adjacent valley. Something still nagged at her, warning of danger, and only when her line of retreat had been secured did she relax for a last look about the Station.

When she was satisfied that nothing important was left undone, she went with Love to the forest where his kind fed. The Deet now treated her as if she were one of their own, so she could see their lithe bodies moving in the trees before they reached today's feeding place. She set Love onto a branch, and he scampered up to communicate with his fellows.

To the normal repertory of hand signals he added several more that she had not seen in all the time she had spent with the Deet. Did they describe the new country he had seen from the flitter, as well as the new people they had found? She suspected as much, for the other Deet seemed excited by his message.

They came down the trees to cluster about her, as well, when Love returned to her. It was as if he understood that they were going away for a long stay. Could he have drawn from her emotional responses, as well as from the trip in the flitter, that inference? The longer she knew the Deet, the more she believed that he could.

She touched furred heads lightly, as the small people came to bid her good-bye. They vibrated gently beneath her fingertips, and she wondered for the first time if that too might be a part of their communications skills. When the last was satisfied, they turned and went back into the trees.

Andraia turned too and carried Love, perched on her shoulder, back toward the Station. While it was still beyond a roll of silver-grassed land, she felt a tingle in the air. Something . . . something danger-

ous . . . was afoot. She flung herself down, holding
Love safely beneath her body.

The sky turned more intensely silver. There
was a crackle like lightning, yet far more potent and
compelling. There was no explosion, yet she knew
that in some way, which those at her level in the
hierarchy of the Service had not been taught, the
Station had been obliterated from Argent. She had
not made any error in working all night.

It was almost night again. If she had remained
in the Station for only a few hours more, she would
have been removed, along with the buildings. Her
hunch had been accurate, and she made a quiet
resolution to pay more heed to such intuitions.

The flitter, in its protected location, was un-
harmed. She would sleep there, and when the sun
rose she would return to her safe haven. She had
been disturbed and suspicious, before. Now she was
angry. Whoever was betraying her Service would find
her a formidable enemy.

27

Andraia found the river valley soothing to her spirit. The fury at her betrayal at the hands of those entrusted with her welfare was eased, as she went about making a home of this new location, by the intense interest of the Ditto, who came to visit her and Love, and by the quiet ripple of the river. She also found herself fascinated by the flyers . . . the few kinds she had noted about the Station had been standard varieties, seed-eaters, predators, and carrion birds, though all had mammalian aspects.

Here she found a myriad of strange sorts of fowl, some of which were aquatic. She had seen tapes of such birds on old Earth, going about their business in intriguing ways. Now she could sit on a flat boulder beside the water and watch pale green flotillas feed among the water plants in the eddies or dive beneath the chill ripples to catch minnow-like swimmers.

Above flitted others of pale blue, silver-gold, and gray-green. She recorded descriptions, habits, and habitats, as well as she could observe them, and found herself feeling more and more attuned to the silent and peaceful world on which she lived.

She had not given up her attempts to communicate directly with the Ditto and Love. However, she was going about it differently. Having set up her computer and monitor in the shelter of her small dwelling, she inserted the discs that could show these alien people something more detailed about her own kind. She showed Love how to change discs, how to activate and deactivate the system. Then she left him alone with the computer for three days.

She returned, of course, at night, but he was usually finished with his day's anthropological study and ready to sleep by the time night fell. She had no idea how he was reacting to what he was learning about mankind. On the fourth evening, she returned to find her shelter overflowing with furred shapes.

The monitor was busy, showing a study of farm life on old Earth. Cattle moved about pastures, in barns, where automatic machines milked, fed, and washed them. Poultry existed in huge factorylike buildings, each fowl confined to a tiny cubicle in which its entire life was spent, until such time as the system required its slaughter.

As Andraia arrived, the disc completed its message, and the screen went dark. There was a flurry of motion as the Ditto conversed among themselves in the dim light. Andraia touched the key that operated the solar-powered illumination system, and her guests blinked owlishly, staring about at each other, at Love, and then at her. They looked stunned. She wondered what else Love might have shown them in the course of the day.

If he had used discs of battle, of cities and

worlds plagued by crime, of the restructuring of planets to human requirements, she was not surprised. Even as she stood there, Love came hurrying to her side and tugged at her pants leg.

She followed as he led her to the console and touched the keys. On the monitor appeared a ship— a Midline cruiser such as her own Service used. The ship was taped from planetside, as it emitted a shuttle from its lower port. The stubby-winged vessel zipped forth, looped into a tight curve, and approached the port, which was visible as an arc of geometric shapes about the bottom of the fish-eye lens that had been used.

Love bounced to touch the shuttle. Then he ran to the door and pointed dramatically toward the flitter, nestled in its concealed spot beneath the trees. Again he came to tug at her leg, looking upward imperatively. One small hand came up, fingers extended on either side, and banked gracefully to a landing on her knee.

A Ditto, small and plump enough to indicate a hidden youngster in a pouch, traced in the dust of the floor a symbol: [\ /] Beside it, she put another: [.\ /.]

Love touched the last symbol, ran to the door, and pointed up into the sky. He flapped his arms energetically and mimicked a swoop toward the ground. Clear enough . . . the second sign was for a bird. There were its feet, plain enough. The first was for the shuttle/flitter, which if not identical were obviously kindred matters.

She smiled with satisfaction. This was the first

breakthrough that could be used as hard evidence. She found her small camera and photographed the symbols in the dust. Tomorrow she would sit with them, leaving her world of birds and animals and river to go on without her. Tomorrow they would find more specifics and begin building the basis for a common system of communication.

28

Busy with her ever-growing store of mutual symbols, Andraia was hardly aware of the passing of weeks. She only realized the lack of storms when Love became extremely nervous and irritable, and she set about finding out the reason at once.

The computer assessed the terrain, the distance from the ocean, and told her what she had begun to suspect. Those severe bouts of weather were deflected from the area in which they now lived by the mountains. Without any danger whatsoever, the Deet was beginning to show signs of emotional stress. Surely the Ditto had found some way in which to satisfy their own longing for adventure.

By now she had enough common hand signs and dot writing at her command to inquire of the Ditto. It wasn't easy, for she had no analog of the treetop rides, but she persevered until the small female responded.

Slash-Dot, as Andraia had named the Ditto, jumped to her furry feet and indicated that Andraia should follow her outside the shelter. She scurried through the forest to a point along the riverbank from which the mountainside could be seen clearly.

Then she patted the jumpsuit pocket in which Andraia's binoculars were kept.

Once she had them focused on the sheer cliff
rising above that first loop of the river, she understood the Ditto version of ride-out-the-storm. Theirs
amounted to scale-the-impossible-cliff. Tiny bodies
were hanging by hands as they swung their legs over
space, leaping from infinitesimal footholds to catch
invisible handholds, or bouncing down the dangerous span, rock to ledge to cranny, with joyful non-
chalance.

Ah! But how could Love, unskilled in rock
climbing, manage to work out his tensions in that
way? She shook her head and sighed. When she
turned toward the tree in which Love sat, morosely
grooming his fur, Slash-Dot followed her and went
up to join her distant kinsman.

There was a flurry of sign language. Love sat
upright and shivered his fur, as he always did when
very excited. He came headfirst down the tree and
ran with Slash-Dot to the river. Once Andraia had
focused the glasses so that he could look through
one side (he was too narrow between the eyes for
anything else) he began to quiver. She knew that he
wanted to go at once to join those happy seekers of
danger on the cliff.

Andraia found that she had no need to worry
about him. The silver-furred people might look like
the sorts of soft toys provided to crèche children to
teach them affection, but they were highly intelligent adults. A delegation of them took Love in hand

162

at once, leading him to a beginner's climb, where some of their young were learning their skills.

Relieved of worry about her companion, Andraia spent days in "talking" with different Ditto individuals and evenings in recording and correlating her findings. She found, within two months, that she had a remarkable amount of data on tape and discs. Enough, she felt certain, to convince the Registrars of Alien Intelligence, if only she could get the material into their hands.

She began to worry, very quietly, about the ship that was supposed to arrive to place another Station, with another caretaker, on Argent. Would the Service risk such a thing? What had that traitor, whoever he might be, back at Base with Fender, told his superiors in order to get them to obliterate an existing, manned Station?

There were other matters too that began to eat at her nerves. Had her direct message gotten through to the Registry? Did anyone suspect that she might have moved from the Station before the signal that destroyed it? And, most worrying of all, how had that destruct signal come through the Shield to activate whatever system must have been built into the installation?

She began to watch the sky for the telltale streak that might indicate the arrival of a shuttle. From time to time she took the flitter up for a scan of the former Station site, though she never approached closely. The valley was still and barren. Not even the scavenger birds approached it.

Spring in the hidden valley was a matter of a slight increase in the warmth of the air, a rise in the water levels from melting snows on invisible peaks. Plants that had seemed as vital as possible put on spurts of growth that staggered her, and the fronds and sprays and tufts of blossom amazed her with their variety. She put it all onto tape. Such a paradisiacal world should not be destroyed, and she was sure that those whose word was final concerning such matters would agree, if only they could see what she saw.

At last there came a time when all her tapes and discs were full. She had even sketched some late-found vertebrates and plants for the record, but she knew that was not evidence. She, as had Love before, became nervous and irritable. The Ditto recognized the problem and hauled her off to the beginners' cliff to climb mountains.

It seemed a modest enough climb, the cliff rising at a slope instead of straight up. Long vertical cracks promised hand and footholds. Love had taken upon himself her instruction, and she followed him up the hummock of pebbles and shards at the bottom and reached the crevice he indicated to her. After that it got much harder; she fell from that seemingly easy surface, on which young Ditto were playing with ease, five times. After that, both she and Love recognized the fact that her larger fingers and toes were going to require larger holds, and the Deet scrambled over the surface of the cliff searching out usable ones for her.

When she reached the top, her fingers were raw

and bloody, her toes felt stubbed past enduring, and she possessed bruises on locations of her anatomy that she had not known existed. But all the young Ditto were lined up at the top, urging her on with sign language, and when she joined them she knew that if they had been capable of cheering they would have done it.

She never achieved the sheer slope that Love had conquered fairly easily. She knew that to attempt it would probably mean to die. But she spent a lot of time on the little slope with the youngsters, and her mind stopped gnawing away at the questions for which she could have no answers.

So it was with a cool head that she saw, one balmy morning, a point of brilliance in the northern sky above the looming peak. A streak—yes. It was a shuttle, without any doubt.

She ran to the river's edge, staring at the point at which the streak had gone behind another mountain. Someone . . . who? . . . had arrived at last!

29

There came a distant crack, like thunder. She turned in her tracks to stare behind her, at the ridge to the south of her position. In a moment the streak was again visible. This time it trailed behind it a blue-gray cloud. Was it afire?

Then she remembered the emergency signal that could be directed to displaced or stranded personnel. Visible from a large part of the planetary surface, it could convey simple messages and directions, stated in a hologram whose size involved hundreds of cubic miles.

The mist spread rapidly, and the shuttle stitched in and out of it several times, providing the magnetic nuclei that formed the communication. Within two hours, the hologram had formed, and Andraia was looking up at a symbol. The logo of the Registry . . . she sighed with relief.

Below it was a stylized map of the continent on which she stood. The dot where the Station had been was a blur of scarlet. Three more symbols were set about that . . . "safety," "return," "consultation."

She reached to touch Love's head. He too was staring into the sky with puzzled eyes. The Ditto— she looked back into the trees—were assessing this new phenomenon with their usual quiet calm.

She turned to the shelter and began to take down its components. As if understanding what this message in the sky meant, the aliens helped as much as they could, packing the smaller equipment neatly into compartments that fitted into the flitter. At the last moment, she paused.

Here was the entirety of her last six months' survey of the people of Argent. If something happened to the flitter as she crossed the country toward the Station, it would all be lost. The records stored with the rescued equipment were very basic stuff, compared to what she now possessed. She needed to secure a good part of it for future reference, if anything untoward should happen. She refused to think of another betrayal . . . her Service was a sound one, under the direct supervision of the Registry. A single traitor was barely thinkable. More than one could not be.

But still she removed one of the sealed pods of records, duplicates made before she realized that she would run out of storage before anyone came, and buried it beneath the tree into which Love had first climbed to talk with his kin. She concealed it well and indicated to the Ditto that this was a very important thing. They would remember, she knew. Any of her kind who came looking for it would be shown where it was concealed.

She looked about the valley where she had lived for so long. She felt a sadness at leaving, but she also felt excitement at being able, now, to convey her knowledge of these new people to those who could protect them.

Love joined her in the cockpit of the flitter, and

all the Ditto in the area retreated to their trees to watch her leave. The craft lifted easily, fully charged with sun energy, and she banked to gain altitude above the river's updraughts. Then they were over the mountain, crossing the range toward the grass-lands.

The hours of travel wearied her. She wanted to unburden herself of this important knowledge at once, to know that Argent would be interdicted to human use until a complete and in-depth study could be done. Love too seemed uneasy, uncurling from his position to gaze down at the land fleeting below them, resettling himself only to move again and again.

The valley of the Station came into sight at last, lifeless and glazed-looking. She could see a shuttle on the grassland beyond a roll of ground, and she began to smile. Even as she did, Love tugged at her sleeve. He was staring at her compellingly.

Was he picking up some emotion from the human beings down there? Were they afraid? Angry? His expression, which she had learned to read with some accuracy, was filled with alarm. Even as she realized that, and before she could ask what was the matter, he pulled at the yoke, putting the flitter into a shallow dive.

That was why the blast of energy overshot them, though it sent the light craft tumbling in the disturbed air of its passage.

Andraia's reflexes corrected the altitude of the flitter, sent them to treetop level behind the rolling terrain, and headed them for a grassy plot she re-called from earlier explorations. Forest came right up to it, and she could pull the flitter into the trees, making it invisible from the air. Either there were many traitors in her Service, or the single one had more influence than she had ever dreamed.

Once she had her vehicle concealed, she set out, Love on her shoulder, for the Station again. Those who had intended to kill her and destroy her information would not, she hoped, expect her to come again, and on foot.

The forest through which they went was conifer, but in a few kliks it began to be interspersed with the hardwoods that grew the fungus the Deet ate. After a time, she began to see silver-furred forms frozen into stillness on branches and in treetops. Only her long practice at detecting their presence allowed her to see them, although Love had begun to quiver when he saw the first group they passed.

They were approaching a thick clump of trees when Love abruptly left her shoulder and scampered up a branch. He joined a group of his kind high above, and Andraia paused to wait for him.

When he came down at last, she was surprised to see a dozen or so of the Deet follow him to the ground. Only when they came near did she recognize some of the individuals she had known during her stay with their kind in the forest. Subtle variations in coloration, size, shapes of heads and bodies, and unobtrusive markings became distinctive, once you knew the small people.

They moved close, patted her pants legs, and fell in behind as she marched on toward the place where her own kind waited to kill her.

30

She had flown farther than she thought. It took most of the next day to cover the ground afoot, but she spent the night on a wide branch, surrounded by Deet. When first light turned the sky to pewter, they were on their way again, and sundown found them gone to ground on a wooded ridge that she had never explored on the southeasterly side of the valley.

A temporary shelter had been erected for the newcomers, though it was not placed on or even very near the spot where the Station had been eliminated. That told her the personnel now in place had detected some dangerous residue there. Nasty business, altogether. She found herself wondering how to deal with those sent by the traitor, misinformed, she was certain, and probably ordered to destroy the local fauna.

By full dark, a ring of power-beams had been placed about the perimeter, and she noted that guard-sensors had been located at frequent intervals. They were afraid. On this most peaceful of worlds, they had only one reason to be, and that was erroneous information given them from the highest possible sources.

Not the Registrars. That she would not believe;

but she began to wonder just what Fender had relayed to his superiors after her transmissions had been received.

When the last of the distant figures had secured themselves in the shelter, Andraia moved forward with the Deet, taking advantage of the low growth of shrubs that edged the wood where they had hidden. She went as near to the encampment as she dared, knowing the sensitivity of the guardians. Then she huddled on the ground with her furry friends and waited for morning and whatever that might bring.

Once it was day again, she used her binoculars to observe the people busy about this proposed Station. She recognized two fellow xenologists, who had trained with her and with Josip. She recognized a pair of crèchemates, zoologists, if she recalled correctly. She had a fleeting moment of sadness, thinking of their Links, still in place and comfortingly secure.

They would know her at once. So would Lilit and Jak. The rest were strangers, though she knew that they were experts in many fields of planetary exploration. They would not be here, otherwise. She did not see Fender or any officer of a rank higher than active Tech-Major. Yet they had tried to blast her flitter from the sky. What sort of monsters had they been told inhabited this world?

She waited, hidden in a clump of shrubbery that had erupted into rampant growth since she left the area. Andraia felt bewildered. What had these people been told about her? That she had been corrupted by some horrendous and inimical local system or plague? If she revealed herself even to those she knew, would they think she had been taken over by some subversive intelligence? That was a danger all xenologists were warned about.

The shuttle was tied down at some distance from the camp. Two sensors stood guard over it, one on either side. If she could get near enough to put one of them out of commission before it erupted into noise and laser blasts, it might be possible to get into the shuttle. Once there, she knew how to send off a signal that no agency of the Interstellar Union could ignore.

Being careful not to stir the growth about her, she lay flat and pulled grass away from a patch of dirt. She dotted into it her pidgin Deet, trying to convey to her small army the thing she wanted to do. She drew painstaking pictures of the sensors, along with the posts on which they were set. She knew there was no way in which she or any large being could approach that shuttle without being blasted, but perhaps these tiny people might manage.

She drew their attention to the direction of the former Station. She indicated the blast of silver light that had devastated that entire valley. The small bright eyes observed her signs and symbols. She thought the Deet understood the danger, yet two made off through the grass, moving so subtly that even she could mark no line of disturbance in the silver-green growth.

For people who had never had occasion to avoid

enemies, they did a creditable job of it. The pair remained below the level of the grass until they came right up to the post. Then one swarmed up it, while the other waved a long stalk of leaves before the round "eye." The guardian blasted away, searing the head from the leaf stalk, while the Deet on top of it disconnected its power source, as she had instructed it by way of a detailed diagram drawn in dirt.

Andraia broke from her cover and ran for the shuttle. The guardian on the other side was shielded from her approach by the body of the craft itself, and it was a moment before anyone in camp noticed her motion. By the time she could hear yells and the searing hisses of hand weapons, she was coding her own access number into the side of the door. In a moment more, she was inside, the door sealed behind her with the command to ignore any access number given it for the next eight hours.

Love had kept pace with her. He was beside her as she made her way forward to the com-unit. He watched with great interest as she coded into the emergency mode a signal that had not, so far as she knew, been sent within living memory.

EMERGENCY. TREACHERY WITHIN. SEND HELP . . . and she typed in, once again, the coordinates of Argent.

Anyone within signaling distance was compelled by interplanetary law to respond, if only by relaying the signal to more accessible units capable of rendering aid. Andraia sank into the seat before the console and felt as if her very bones were melting with the release of stress.

Love was signaling from the window to a row of Deet below, sheltered from view of those in camp by the shuttle's bulk. She pushed her friend aside and signaled an urgent MOVE AWAY TO SAFETY! They evidently recalled the blasts from the guardian. The group retreated into the grass and became invisible.

31

It was the longest day Andraia remembered
living through. Though she found much of interest
inside the shuttle to occupy herself, she kept watching the monitors for any approaching craft. Somewhere out there was a mother ship, which was
certainly in touch with those in the camp. They
would send help, if another shuttle was aboard.

She could not, however, think that anyone
would try to damage the shuttle in which she sat.
Shuttles were the workhorse lifelines of planetary
exploration. The thought of attacking one to damage
it would be as foreign to anyone in her Service as
would destroying a world on which there was an
intelligent species.

Ha! she thought.

The morning warmed into noon. The sky
turned silver-gilt as the sun burned away most of the
mist from the valleys. Then it went almost pinkish
as clouds came out of the northwest, heralding one
of the regular coastal storms. By late afternoon, the
wind was rising, rain was beginning to mist across
the valleys in trailing folds, and the shuttle seemed
as isolated as a cave in a wilderness.

A sudden beep from the com-unit woke Andraia

from a light doze, and she sat upright and reached for the keys. INCOMING INCOMING STAND BY scrolled down the console. As she waited, the message began to arrive.

> PRIORITY ONE, AUTHORITY REGISTRY OF ALIEN INTELLIGENCES, HALT ALL, REPEAT ALL, ACTIVITIES RE ARGENT, FAUNA OF, STATION LOCATED ON, ATTENDANT ONSITE. REPRESEN-TATIVES ARRIVING NINETEEN HUNDRED HOURS STANDARD. STAND BY FOR ARRIVAL. OUT.

Andraia stood straight and stared up through the transparent dome, scanning the streaming sky for any sign. But of course there was none. Nineteen hundred hours standard would come just before dawn, Argent time. The storm would be doing its worst by then, she suspected. Confusion was going to reign for a while. She hoped that the group in the camp had also received the message on its smaller com-system.

She went back into the cramped temporary quarters provided for crew and passengers. She found a bunk that seemed less stony than most and sank onto it, pulling over her the light thermal covering. Love curled against her side, as she slid into sleep. She was totally relaxed for the first time in a very long while, and she dived deep.

She woke to Love's tugging. He had a strand of hair, and he was doing his best to wake her without really hurting her. She struggled to a sitting position and yawned.

"What?" she said, still groggy with sleep. Then she remembered.

A quick dash through the Cleanser unit and a bite of concentrate brought her back to herself enough to check the time and the weather. It was pouring rain now, the wind buffeting the distant forest, just visible in lightning flashes. The shuttle, heavy and solid, sat like a rock, undisturbed by the tumult about it. The camp shelter, however, was flapping, one edge having torn free of its stays. Small figures were bumbling about, trying to secure it again.

The faint tinge of gray that heralded dawn on Argent would not be visible in the storm. Yet Andraia had been on-planet long enough to get the feel of just-before-dawn. It was time for the RAI Reps to arrive.

Even as she watched, a brilliant light shone from overhead. One of the Black Hole class shuttles settled majestically to the grass on the other side of the encampment. The people stopped struggling with their shelter and turned, lining up with military precision, even though the wind kept buffeting them almost off their feet.

A burst of sparks told Andraia that a Field had formed, enclosing both the other shuttle and the camp. That meant that she could safely leave her own shelter and take the canister of tape that she had brought from her flitter to those who were now in charge of this world.

She rummaged in the supply cupboard, finding an all-weather garment that covered her from head to toe. She tucked Love into one vast inner pocket and the canister into another. Then she unsealed the shuttle and dropped onto the sodden grass below.

No sooner had she alighted than she felt rather than saw movement about her. The Deet? How had they managed in the storm . . . and then she remembered. This was something that would appeal to their daring natures. She did not object when the entire group, now considerably more than a dozen, followed her toward the glimmer that was the Field.

Her feet squished into mud and blown-down grasses as she made her way to the edge of the shielded spot. The Field being designed, in such circumstances, to keep out weather, not people, she penetrated it with minimal effort and went forward toward the group standing in earnest talk beside the limp shelter.

Someone off to the side spotted her and cried out. The group that had tried to blast her seemed to cringe, as if expecting her to do something monstrous. The four people who had arrived in the Black Hole shuttle stood erect, staring at her with interest.

"Andraia-Link-Josip, I presume," said the leathery-skinned man who seemed to be in charge.

His gaze dropped to her feet. His eyes widened, and the other two men and the woman stepped forward as if pulled on wires.

"And friends?" he asked, his tone wry.

"Yes, sir. I have also brought tapes and discs, though the discs are not with me at this moment, to demonstrate the intelligence and creativity of this new species of intelligent being. In addition, I have a hidden deposit that includes even more material. I was not certain of my welcome"—she glanced aside at the contingent from the Service—"when I came back to the site of the old Station."

The skinny woman wearing a major's cluster was staring at her despairingly. Andraia smiled reassuringly. She had assumed all along that this group had been misinformed.

"That is why I landed the flitter and approached on foot. I knew that someone back at Base had misinterpreted, accidentally or on purpose, my reports concerning the Deet. I knew that whoever was on site must be terrified because of that. The Deet put the guardians out of commission, after I showed them how, and I took refuge in the shuttle."

"It seems that there has been a real foul-up at Base," said the Registrar. "I am Como. Kinnit, Saver, Delk, and I are assigned the task of sorting it out. But first we had to make certain that no erroneous orders could result in damage to the people of Argent. You have our profound thanks for preventing a terrible disaster."

Como gave a jerk of his chin, and the ranked Service people relaxed and went about putting their shelter into order. The four Registrars beckoned to Andraia and her Deet contingent. Before she could move, Love bounced forward and climbed the Registrar's leg. He settled onto the man's shoulder, peered into his ear, cocked his head to examine the insignia on his collar.

"I see that this is a very informal world," said Kinnit, her tone dry. "We don't seem to awe your companions a bit."

Andraia laughed. "Where there is no danger, there can be no fear," she said. "Here there is no danger of any kind, other than that of storms or rock-climbing. They do that, you know, just for excitement . . ." She was almost chattering as they moved back into the huge shuttle.

Como was the last to enter the craft. He seemed to be feeling the comforting quiver of Love's fur against his neck. "There is much to learn here," he said.

"The people of Argent are empathic," said Andraia. "That is what Love felt that brought him to me . . . he felt my pain at losing my Link. He came to ease it." She almost forgot and added that he had felt the terror of those in the new camp and saved her from destruction.

The canister was handed over and its contents copied at once. Then Andraia was sent into the lounge and handed hot soup, food of many kinds, and the sort of coddling she had never known before.

32

OVERRIDE ALL PREVIOUS ORDERS.

ARGENT, SECTOR 11837, LATERAL THREE, DIAGONAL ELEVEN, STARGRID NINE.

ASSIGNED TO ANDRAIA-LINK-JOSIP (delete) 0423381 PERMANENT LIAISON, in charge of all study groups to be sent for in-depth investigation of sapient inhabitants, flora, and fauna.

BY AUTHORITY OF REGISTRY OF ALIEN INTELLIGENCE.

ADDITIONAL ORDER: ARREST SOONEST ALEX FENDER, COM OFFICER; KRAL LIMING, OFFICER IN CHARGE BASE. CHARGE CONFLICT OF IN-TEREST, ENDANGERING INTELLIGENT SPECIES. ATTEMPTED MURDER, DESTRUCTION OF SERV-ICE PROPERTY, PERJURY IN ISSUANCE OF OR-DERS TO EMERGENCY PERSONNEL.

VIA REGISTRY COM-LINK: BYPASS NORMAL SU-PERLIGHT.

The confusion was over, and Argent was quiet again. The breeze sighed inaudibly through the trees, and the Deet went about their business in their usual silence. Andraia, in her newly constructed Shelter, found herself reveling in her solitude, which was relieved only by the frequent visits of Love.

Other people would come, in time, when the problems on Base were sorted out. The guilty officers were standing their ground firmly, like true military personnel, taking all the heat that should have gone to those above them in the chain of command. Some superior had undoubtedly said to them: This is unofficial, of course, but you do need to do something about that madwoman on Argent. She is about to destroy our opportunity to test the new weapons on that world, and it is the most suitable one we've found.

Nobody admitted that, of course. But Andraia had lived all her life in a military context, and she knew how such things worked. Fender and Liming would be court-martialed, reprimanded, possibly even imprisoned—and they would disappear into the hands of the military, which would probably hold them for a while and then slip them unobtrusively into other positions where they needed loyal subordinates who didn't mind doing nasty jobs.

The Registry was already organizing a schedule of investigation for Argent. They had assured Andraia that her judgment would be their guideline, for she was the only human being who knew anything at all about the Deet and their kindred.

That would be a great responsibility—the silver-furred people would rest in her hands, for better

or for worse. A world, once discovered to have intelligent life upon it, could not be undiscovered again,
and her friends were going to have to learn to accom-
modate themselves to the prying of human beings.
She would give everything she had to the task of
keeping that from upsetting their lives more than
necessary.

Perhaps she might live her entire life here on
Argent, working out the intricacies of the culture of
these small people. No longer did the thought of
alien beings terrify her, and she knew that she could
go wherever she was assigned, but she hoped fer-
vently that this would be her permanent station.

And yet she hoped too that one day others of
her kind might return to Thryllia, which was still
interdicted. She understood, now, the cause of Josip's
death. Others could deal, from a basis of that understanding, with the Thryll.

She knew that she would not be one of those.
She had lost her life's companion, but with great
good luck she had found her life's work to take his
place.

Few were so fortunate, she thought, greeting
Love, as she opened her door onto a new day on the
silver world.